BlackpoolCouncil

A 1
2/11

D1680989

Please return/renew this item
by the last date shown.

To renew this item go to :
www.blackpool.gov.uk/libraries
or phone : **01253 478070**

For you, set your soul free!

R M A Wulf

I Am Therian

AUSTIN MACAULEY PUBLISHERS™

LONDON • CAMBRIDGE • NEW YORK • SHARJAH

A CIP catalogue record for this title is available from the British Library.

ISBN 9781528907125 (Paperback)
ISBN 9781528907132 (Hardback)
ISBN 9781528907149 (E-Book)

www.austinmacauley.com

First Published (2019)
Austin Macauley Publishers Ltd
25 Canada Square
Canary Wharf
London
E14 5LQ

To my lovely mother, the honest voice of both doubt and reason, I did it! Please read it now. To my partner-in-crime Ruby A River for being as excited about the characters as I have been, for believing in the story I wanted to tell and being the first to read the manuscript' and informing me the romance needed more depth. My 'idiot' best friend for pushing me to pursue this dream as though it were his own and being with me at every step of this adventure. To my three outrageously sarcastic and witty brothers, my sister-in-law and to the two little humans who have stolen my heart completely, Ayaana Skye and Isaiah. To M Scott; to Janet R, my dear friend who has confidence in my ability to achieve anything my heart desired; to Rimsha, Heather and Junaid; to my favourite K-Pop idol group; and finally to all the staff at Austin Macauley who helped my dream become a reality.

Chapter One

My pale blue dress was torn to shreds; my bare feet and legs were battered with cuts and bruises. Running through the trees I focused on the urgency in his voice.

"Please Mina, keep running. Don't look back, don't turn around, don't get caught. Run!" The voice rang loud in my ears.

Uneven shallow breaths escaped my lips as I took a tumble, stopping myself at the edge of a cliff, and it dawned on me that I have nowhere to go.

"Nowhere to run now, little miss, no one to save you," shouted one, followed by howls of laughter. My eyes streamed and I realised I may not see him again; that thought alone was scarier than any death coming for me. I saw the glint of metal as one of the men charged towards me, and closing my eyes, I prepared myself for the worst. Instead, I ended up being tackled to the ground from a different direction, the air knocked out of me.

"I've got you, don't worry."

I opened my eyes and couldn't stop my heart from smiling, his piercing red eyes scorched my soul, as he spluttered blood before leaping over the edge of the cliff, taking me with him...

Jumping up in a cold sweat, I waited for my eyes to adjust to the darkness. They finally landed on my best friend's face. He was asleep in a chair next to my bed, his large frame looking cramped and uncomfortable in the space it was in. I instantly recalled the last few weeks. I was taking time out from my boyfriend and I had to leave my job due to the onset of stress that led to me fainting at random moments.

Jesse McGuire and I had been together for almost three years on and off. It was a chaotic relationship, but I kept taking him back because I blindly loved him. He was meant to be the guy I was to spend the rest of my life with. Jesse wasn't good with words. He generally struggled to tell people what he thought and felt, but he tried to be open with me. He let me in and showed me a side of him that was well hidden behind his macho, funny guy persona, and that's why I fell for him. We both struggled to connect to others, him emotionally and me physically.

I thought we balanced each other out.

I met Jesse through Clay (Alexander Clayton), my best friend and confidante. We both worked at an arts studio, me behind reception and him as an artist. Jesse wasn't the first person I met from Clay's group and we didn't click right away; to be frank, I couldn't really stand him. He was boisterous and self-absorbed while I was shy and reserved.

Clay looked out for me like an older brother and we became close right away. He always tried to make sure I was okay. We have an inside joke that he's my 'shield', as he protects me from everything, whether it be an insect or a boy.

When I met Clay, I had woken up from a coma. I couldn't remember anything but distorted images. When he heard all this, he changed and used it as an excuse to be overly protective. He was always pointing out how naive I truly was. He had always warned me about his friends, making it a habit to tell me not to 'trust boys', even him.

I remember the night Jesse and I fell out. He had dropped me off across the road from my parents' semidetached. The dark night was crisp and quiet. The streetlamps bounced off the sign for Victoria Crescent as I walked into the warmth of number seven and crept up to my room where Clay lay in wait.

"Where have you been?" his voice came out of nowhere, making me jump out of my skin.

"Sheesh Clay," I almost cursed. I nudged him with as much power as I could muster, catching him off guard. He landed on his backside and sat glaring at me. He should have been grateful that he landed on a fluffy carpet and not on the wooden floorboards. I smirked and stuck my tongue out. I had made sure that my room was the essence of comfort, all vintage in style but warm and cosy.

"In the five years I've known you, Mina, you haven't uttered a single curse word. I'm still trying my luck to push you over that edge," he said, dusting off his backside.

"Uh huh, keep trying my love, you'll get there one day," I laughed.

"Who were you with at this time of night?" he asked, glancing at me. I knew he already knew the answer. I stayed silent; he didn't need me to spell it out.

"You know, I've always tried to keep you from getting hurt, Mina. So, I'm just a bit mad right now 'cause you're going to end up learning the hard way." He looked deflated as he took a seat on the end of my bed and ran his hands through his hair.

"Clay, I'm a big girl. I know how to look after myself." I tried to smile but the look in his eyes threw me.

"Have you ever looked at his phone or social media accounts, or are you just scared of what you'll find? He's my friend, but I know what kind of a piece of shit he really is. That's why I've warned you time and time again. Do you think I want to watch your heart break? Every time I look at Jesse, I want to put his head through a wall. I've never felt like that before. Why do you make me feel like this?" He was angry; I'd never seen him angry before. Everyone suffers heartbreak, but he was going a bit over the top.

"I don't question what you do with girls, Clay, why do you think you can question me?" Leaping from the bed, he was literally a centimetre from my face. I held my breath.

"I'm not questioning you; I'm just telling you, you deserve better! Why hasn't he made you guys an official thing? Why doesn't he show his affection for you in front of us? I may date a lot but I'm not an ass. The girls know I'm not looking for anything serious. But Jesse, he makes you feel like you're the only one, but you're just another notch he wants to add to his bed post, another girl he can throw away after he's done with you. Don't you get it?" My hand reacted; before I could stop myself, I felt the sting from the slap on my palm. How do I tell my best friend there's something wrong with me, that I'm broken, and Jesse understands? I didn't think Jesse would cheat on me, but can I blame him if he did? There were always seeds of doubt in my mind, but now Clay was forcing me to face them, and I was not ready.

Clay was left shaking as I tried to digest what he had said and the fact that I had just slapped my best friend. He wiped away the tears that had escaped, and that was my breaking point. I collapsed into his arms and cried.

I don't know how long we'd been standing but my tears had subsided and I was aware of my phone buzzing.

. Jesse. Clay stopped me.

"Don't answer. He doesn't deserve it." Looking at my best friend I tried to smile, assuring him I'd be okay, as his ashy brown hair fell over his green eyes. His full lips tried to return my smile but were left incomplete. I noticed the dusting of stubble on his strong jawline, further adding to his masculinity.

When I first saw Clay, I remember being attracted to him, but he'd always had a flutter of girls around him. It was way too much hard work for me, and I eventually got over it. Then I met Jesse, my distraction. He was so cocky, always letting me know I wouldn't find a better guy than him and that no guy would understand my repulsion at physical contact.

"Clay, I need to face this. I'll ask him where we are headed and then make my decision," I said, patting his arm and then walking to my phone.

"Do you want me to leave?" he asked, but I shook my head. I knew I wouldn't be able to go through with it if he wasn't there to witness it.

Taking a deep breath, I answered. "Hey, did you get home okay?" My voice was hoarse from crying.

"I did. What's wrong with your voice?" He noticed little things, did that count?

"Jesse?"

"Yes, Mina." I could hear the sleep in his voice.

"Where is this going?" The silence dragged, and I felt my heart thumping loud.

"Are you there?"

"I'm here." He sounded distant, as he usually did whenever this topic came up.

"Well?" My legs shook, and the temperature dropped. I sat down on the floor.

"I don't know where this is going." I unconsciously started to rock back and forth, shivering. Clay sat behind me and wrapped his arm around my shoulders. I felt myself getting angry.

"So, I'm a time pass kinda girl, someone to turn to when no other girl takes your call?" I couldn't hide how hurt I was.

"Don't be stupid; you're not time pass."

"Then what am I to you? You've known for a while that my feelings for you have developed and yet you're acting like this is nothing." My stupid tears rolled on cue.

"Your feelings are your feelings. They have nothing to do with me." I cut him off, what more could I say? It's the same old story; we always fell out like this.

I couldn't do much but cry. I let it all out. It felt like my world was crumbling and taking my heart with it. The sobs just kept coming. Throughout my ugly crying, Clay just sat still, keeping his arms around me. When it started to subside, this guy, who's been my friend for five years, lifted me up like nothing and put me to bed. Clay just walked over to my couch with a blanket and lay down without a word. That was the first time he'd stayed at my place.

Since our last conversation, Jesse had made no effort to fight for us. I was trying to be objective and see things from his perspective; was I pushing him into a relationship that wouldn't give him satisfaction?

I'd gone through every excuse in the book to find a way back to him. I constantly checked his social media and freaked out when I clicked on our chat and it would show him online, as if he could see I was looking at our chats.

There was a playful knock on my bedroom door… It was Clay announcing his presence, like he didn't climb in through my window on a regular basis. He had been lifting my spirits, so the heartache wasn't that bad. Clay had made sure my mind was occupied till I'd passed out.

I opened the door, only for my five-foot-two frame to be towered over by his six-foot-plus body of a giant. He flashed me his million-dollar smile.

"I hope you're hungry, weirdo," he winked. He had popcorn under his arm, a plate of cheesy salsa nachos in his hand, and on the other side was a huge tub of chocolate brownie and fudge sauce ice cream, and a paper bag with my favourite restaurant's logo on it. "Spicy fire peri peri chicken!" My mouth watered just thinking about it.

"Mina, close your mouth, you're drooling." He gently headbutted me into the room.

I helped him lay out the table and we got comfy on my humongous couch. I passed him the remote as our entertainment for the night was waiting. Taking a bite out of my spicy chicken, I let the tantalising lime dressing on the salad and spices make me hmmm. I was distracted a little by Clay's sigh. He covered his face with his hands as he just realised how we'd be spending the next couple of hours and hated it. We spent the night eating, pulling faces and play fighting, undisturbed.

I woke up as a draught passed over my legs, partly because I was uncomfortable. I became restless as I figured out that I was .sleeping on Clay. He had somehow become a human pillow. Random thoughts ran through my mind, like why didn't he put me to bed like usual, or even why didn't I haul my backside to bed, regardless of how comfy my couch was? I needed to get off him before he woke up and things got extremely weird, so I ran to my bed.

Now here he was, sleeping beside me. I placed a blanket on my best friend and climbed back into bed. Jesse fleetingly crossed my mind and for a moment I thought I had fallen for the wrong guy, before my eyes gave in.

In the morning, I rushed to get into the shower. I didn't even look to see if I had woken him with all the tumbling gymnastics I was participating in. Quiet doesn't go hand in hand with a walking hazard, and being clumsy is second nature to me.

I found myself blushing profusely with the picture that my mind was painting as a reminder of last night.

Awkward. Refreshed, I headed back to find Clay sitting down in a tidy room.

"Morning, Mina… Why are you looking at me like that?" he asked, raising a brow.

"You tidied up!" My room always has things lying around, so being able to see my fluffy rug in its entirety is different, to say the least.

"Wash up and come down for breakfast. You want coffee?" I asked.

"Coffee would be great." Clay and I both had an unwavering affection for our coffee fix. At breakfast, my parents and Clay chatted away. I just watched. It felt like a family and I liked Clay being part of this one.

He'd not had much of his own and it felt as if I was giving something back to him as a thank you for always being there for me. On his way out, he whispered: "You've got this; remember your worth." He knew I was going to message Jesse as my parents were heading out too.

I went back up to my room, switching my phone on. It pinged and pinged and pinged… Multiple messages and voicemails flew in.

"I was harsh, I'm sorry."
"Why is your phone off?"
"You know you need me, Mina."
"Just one message, let me know you're okay and that we're good."
"I made an idiot move, and I'm sorry."
"You can't find better than me."
"Let's talk at least."
"Mina…"

This is what I dealt with all the time. He didn't know what he wanted, and I deserved better.

I sent a quick reply. *"Come to mine. We need to talk."*

I needed to look somewhat presentable. I had a wardrobe full of clothes but nothing nice to wear. Clothes flew everywhere, goodbye carpet.

Throwing on a white, knee-length skater skirt and baggy knit jumper with basic makeup, I released my hair from its bun and shoved everything back in the wardrobe, just in time for the doorbell to ring.

I let Jesse in, without even looking back at him as he followed me back up to my room.

"Hi…" is all he managed to say.

"Hey…" I took my time to look up at him. He looked a little dishevelled, which honestly made me smile on the inside…to know it had been hard on him too.

"How have you been?" he asked, watching me intently.

"I've been better than I thought." He nodded.

I never thought I would feel uncomfortable around Jesse, but there's always a first. The rain outside is usually a comforting sound but today it was making me anxious.

"We can't keep doing this, Jesse. I'm always the one hurting. Alone. You used our friendship and my feelings for you to fill your needs. I don't know if it's ever occurred to you how much you're hurting me. In our relationship, I've been in love with you at some point or another and I thought you felt the same, but you don't, and I can't make you feel that… I don't want to end up hating you when we've been friends. So, I think we should just walk away and not contact each other, so that if we ever meet in the future we can at least be civil." I looked at him, feeling both emotional and relieved to be able to say what I needed to without crying. He just stared at the ground.

The rain hitting my window and the ticking of the grandfather clock in the corner filled the silence. We were breathing in sync; minutes passed. I stood at a distance, not knowing if I wanted to hug him or beat him. How was he so calm?

He followed me around and made me feel like he was the .one who would change things for me. Why wasn't he falling apart? The overwhelming sensation of the end had its grip on me, stopping me from speaking further. I knew the second my mouth opened it would all be over. I would succumb to my need for him. I could hear the cracks in my heart ringing in my ears.

"I'm sorry, Mina, I never thought this day would come." He spoke first; his voice sounded broken as he turned away.

My heart was racing, dizzy and nauseous, and my balance started failing. Not wanting to show my weakness, I reached out to the side and held tight onto the chair in front of me.

Please look at me, the thought ran through my mind before I could register the tears streaming down my face.

"I'm sorry if I ever hurt you. I'll delete your number, so I'm not tempted to message you."

I couldn't even bring myself to speak, memories of us rushed through my mind. I wanted to tell him not to leave me; he didn't need to prove that he loved me. I just needed him.

Without looking back, he had gone. My door closed after him, shocking me back to reality, and I ran. I could hold on to him. He'd stay. I didn't care if we had no future, I didn't care how many times he broke my heart, I didn't care. I didn't…

I tried to follow him…rushing down the stairs on to the street, ignoring the blaring horns, my hair all over my face, my eyes following my body 360 degrees. Blinded by lights, and for the shortest moment, I was sure I saw the eyes that had previously haunted my dreams. Red, angered.

Jesse's POV

Seeing her again after what seemed forever almost tore me to pieces. I know what she's going to do. I have always tried to keep her at arm's length, so that I could complete the task at hand. No feelings were meant to be involved, my parents had already fixed my fate, they call it a marriage of convenience. One that will pave my future. I didn't come to Mina for love; I came for information.

She's beautiful. Looking at her now, it seems like she'll cope. Me on the other hand, I couldn't eat or sleep, constantly hoping that she would call me back even though I know others are watching. I can't let them know that I have fallen for a non-spirit. I would be disowned.

She says what she needs to, and I know I must leave. I can't look at her and not tell her that I've betrayed her. This girl has my heart in the palm of her hands and she doesn't even know it. She shouldn't know it. I mumble my sorry excuses and run to get out of there as all I can think of is to beg her to give me a real chance because I think I'm in love with her. The one thing I needed to know, I didn't get the answer to.

Who is Kang to her?

Chapter Two

"You told me she would be safe, away from us, and that I should trust you." A familiar voice filled my ears.

"I thought she would be; you said she was fine the last few years." A girl?

"She almost died, River. If I didn't get there on time, every bone in her body would have shattered," anguish filled his voice; it hurt me a little.

"I can see that. I've been the one stitching you back together. No one told you to use your body to shield her, what if something had happened to you, then what? She wouldn't have had a chance to get to know who you were, would she have forgiven herself, after everything?" She sounded annoyed.

"I vowed to protect her, remember? I'd die for her, but you know that already. It's time for her return. So, make her stay, don't give her an option out, use whatever method you can. She needs to be where we can see her."

Why was his voice familiar?

"Get your hands off me and keep it down, her sedatives are wearing off." The girl sounded familiar too. My eyes felt like .they were glued shut and my throat was on fire. I needed a drink and something for the agonising pain; what had happened? Prying apart my eyelids, everything was a little fuzzy. I was under a gorgeous night sky with glowing bright white stars everywhere. Trying to sit up, I saw two people a few metres away. I couldn't focus on them as the pain was taking over, and looking down, I could see wires in my arm. I was at a hospital? I pulled at one of them, only to receive a loud beeping sound. There was movement in front as the two figures rushed towards me, but before I could get to see them, everything went black.

I was in darkness, unable to see, speak or move. I remembered the lights from when I followed Jesse. I wasn't dead as I could feel the warmth of a wash cloth. I was being wiped down. Someone kept fixing my pillow, the bed, my hair and everything else. Sometimes I heard voices, sitting by my side, talking to me. Parts were clear, the female voice, the male voice saying he was here for me. He came and sat with me for hours, not saying anything, just holding my hand. At one point I heard the girl tell him that I'd be fine, and he replied, "I know, she's a fighter." His voice stirred something in me that I couldn't understand. I couldn't really define reality because when I was alone, in silence, he lay down with me, pulling me closer and just wrapped his arms around me. Was it weird that I didn't even think of fighting him off? Not that I could move anyway. But his touch doesn't make me sick or give me a mental breakdown. It felt nice and comforting, without the everyday sounds my imagination kept feeding my fear. I've never been a fan of the dark. Time passed slowly.

It had been a few hours since someone had sat with me—the silence was a reminder of the eeriness of scary movies where the girl is unable to wake up, all alone. For someone who slept with a night light on, I couldn't begin to explain what this constant darkness was like. I was always scared and I'm not even sure what of, just that I was. When I could hear the hustle and bustle of people, I was afraid of being with strangers. When I was alone, I was scared of just that, being alone. Where were my parents and Clay?

The feeling right now was different. Think horror movie anxiety. I was on edge, heart palpitations, sweating and all those things that come with intense fear. Whatever 'medication' I'd been under was losing its effect and I could feel some of the pain, but not as terrible as the first time I came around. I could wiggle my fingers and toes; I tried to regain some feeling through small movements. I was distracted by a grunting sound. Initially, I thought I'd misheard, but then my spine started to tingle and the hairs on my body rose. I honestly thought there was someone in the room with me, in the silence, in the shadows.

I couldn't see in the darkness and I didn't have enough strength to lift my neck or sit up! My breathing escalated and the mental clarity I had just gained didn't seem as appealing anymore. I wanted to submerge back into complete darkness with no sense of anything. The fear kept intensifying as the moments dragged by slowly.

What should I do?

My mind suddenly gave me a lesson on intense flash photography, not helping the situation. I just let the nauseating feeling take over. I thought I was going to die! My head was ready to explode, my body was shivering uncontrollably, and the bed was drenched with sweat. There was someone in the room with me, I could feel it. Their presence was too close for comfort and I could hear their breathing getting closer, deep and heavy, blanketing the silence.

Shock ran through my body as the feeling of wet fur made its way up my leg. Screaming in silence, I felt the wetness of my tears make their way down either side of my face. The weight of whatever it was pressed against my bed; it was huge. No sound left my mouth. Someone, anyone, please help me! In that moment, the room echoed with a deep rumbling sound, shaking everything, including me. From a low vibration to a powerful, electrifying growl, covering my entire body with goosebumps.

For some inexplicable reason, the fear that had engulfed me started to fade away. I had gone from trembling to being calm. What followed I can't even begin to explain, it sounded like an action sequence you'd hear whilst watching a movie, a full-on brawl, with things smashing and crashing. The sounds were coming from all directions, so I can only assume I was in the centre of it.

I was suddenly knocked out of bed and onto the hard, cold floor. Within seconds, a deep animalistic screech had filled the room before the sound of glass shattering brought about silence. I lay there…helpless, on my stomach, with my cheek going numb from lying on the solid floor. I felt a blow to my head when I landed.

The room went silent for a while, till I heard footsteps rushing towards me. I was lifted into the air and I could feel the warmth of a man, his chest, well defined and strong. His scent was smoky and sweet, captivating my senses. My body and mind focused on his every sound and movement. He lay me down on the bed, kissed my forehead and disappeared, leaving a longing that redefined my perspective on everything I've known of myself. Who was he? I woke up completely relaxed. What a weird dream I'd had last night. I saw blurred circles when I opened my eyes and gave them a little rub. I came face to face with a girl, leaving me confused. Her big, round, brown eyes were focused on me and she had a worried scowl. Her skin was flawless, glowing, with red plump lips that complimented her deep olive skin.

"Mina, are you okay?" She was the girl behind the voice, the one who'd been caring for me. I thought I had dreamt of her.

"Um, I'm okay," I replied, clearing my throat to help the sound come out better. As she helped me to sit up, it dawned on me that I wasn't at home or at the hospital. Looking around, I saw everything had been completely trashed. The room itself was grand, minus all the broken furniture. The walls were an off cream colour that led up to the highest ceiling ever. The sky I saw when I first woke up was a very intricate mural of painted stars. The bed I was lying in was for more than two people. I couldn't get over the size of this room. I felt small.

My eyes landed on my hands and I noticed the red stains all over me. Blood covered the sheets. Checking my body for signs of injury or the slightest pain, I touched my head where I'd fallen, but there was nothing. "Don't worry, it's not your blood, I've checked you over. Imagine my shock coming in to see you this morning lying in blood. I've wiped off as much as I could without disturbing you. I don't know what happened last night, I'm sorry, I shouldn't have left you alone," she said, watching me cautiously.

"Where am I?" I croaked.

She stood up and tapped her foot. She was hesitant, pacing back and forth.

"This is going to sound…somewhat crazy! Are you sure you want to do this now?" she exhaled.

"Who are you?" She sounded familiar, but it was not a face I remembered.

"I'm River, River Castillo," she smiled.

"River, where am I? How did I get here? What about my parents? I can recall being hit by a car or something but that's it, and then last night, I was attacked by some…thing…and someone saved me…"

I knew I was rambling, but I went from chasing after Jesse to being here. Wherever here was.

"First, don't worry, breathe. We have time to cross one bridge at a time. Your parents know you're safe. I made sure Tyler spoke to your friend Clay. You got into an accident. If Tyler hadn't brought you here, we could have lost you. You've been in and out of consciousness for just a few weeks, and thankfully we medicated you so that your body could fully heal as you tried getting up after three days, and that would have caused further damage. Tyler brought you here because he was worried and didn't know what else to do."

I've missed weeks of my life?

"Who's Tyler? Where is here? Why didn't he take me to a hospital? That's the most logical thing to do."

She just smiled.

"Which do you want answering first? For someone who has been through quite an ordeal, you're asking the wrong questions. You should be asking things like was there any serious damage?"

"These are important questions and I asked them because I feel fine."

"Tyler is my friend. Well, he's more your friend than anything, as that's how I got to know him. He is a jack-of-all-trades; the guy can do anything he puts his mind to. That is why he is one of Clandestine's biggest superstars. He has international fans and is good at his role of being the leader of a K-pop idol group, but that's not all. He also doubles that with hunting down rogues." River lost me after K-pop idol. What is an international superstar doing around me? And more to the point, if he was my friend, I think I would know. There are no Tylers in my life.

"Rogues?" It's not a term I've heard a lot of and it somehow didn't fit our conversation.

"Rogues are defectors from Clandestine. They grew up learning the same values as us but were somehow turned along the way. They no longer seek out goodness in humanity, they thrive off power and ego and the things that fuel those, such as fear and money. There a more of us than there are rogues though, and we try hard to ensure the safety of those who don't know we exist, the non-spirits. At Clandestine, you don't just train in the arts, you also train to protect the lives of those different to us. Our skill sets and our bloodlines help us to do just that." Her words seemed to be too rehearsed and far-fetched to just be accepted at face value.

"Back to Tyler. He doesn't care about much of anything other than his work, both as a hunter and idol. He hates politics and doesn't care enough to trust all people. As a hunter at Clandestine, he's known as the stone heart. He is emotionless and cold and downright rude at times. People fear him as he's the type to kill without hesitation. However, over the last few years, I've understood that he is fiercely protective when it comes to you and there is no emotion you don't invoke in him. His fans also have softened him, and he wouldn't let any harm come to them. Even though his roles contrast, being an idol makes him happy. He loves to make his fans smile, which is weird because when you see him outside of that environment, he's like two different people. In terms of Clandestine, do you want to know the truth or the public version of us?" She's lost me again.

"Public version? Let me guess, it's a magic school?" I said, rolling my eyes. She just laughed.

"I see your accident didn't knock the sarcasm right out of you. It's been lonely without you the last few years." She walked towards me and gave me a tight hug, whilst I feigned hurt and heartbreak over her comment. "Erm, this is a tad too long… it's a little…you know, weird, you just holding me. Please stop!" It wasn't bad, it was familiar, but I didn't really do mushy moments; it was left out of my genetic makeup.

"River, just tell me the facts, so I can get my head around it quicker. Rip it off like a band aid. I feel like I can't differentiate between what is real and what's imaginary right now, so I need facts." The whole thing just feels surreal and the more River adds, the more like fiction it seems to be.

"Okay, everything I'm gonna say now is going to sound a little crazy, but hear it all out before you ask questions." She gave me a weird look and patted my head before taking a seat on my bed and holding my hand, like all the things she'd been saying up till now had been sane.

"Clandestine is known as an arts academy worldwide, but it's more than that. It's an internationally led therian base that's controlled by a select number of representatives from different countries, who are known as the 'chargé d'affaires'. We consist of therian musicians, models, dancers and actors, anything in the arts world. But that's not all we do; our main goal is to protect humanity and bring balance to a world falling apart. We work to remove the deviants who are trying to cause chaos around the world by firstly, showing non-therians that they aren't alone and secondly, trying to create conflict so that war will erupt everywhere, causing an imbalance in the world, leading to natural disasters. There is only so much that this planet can take.

"Clandestine contains people who are somewhat different, so we're seen as a threat. No one likes change or things they don't know or understand. So they become defensive or incite conflict as a form of protection which, let's face it, doesn't bring about world peace.

"A few years ago, our Royal family were all assassinated. That is when the chargé d'affaires came into power. The members of the Royal family kept us all in check, as they had a hierarchical power that affected us all. It's to do with the ancestries and bloodlines. An understandable comparison would be with wolves: an alpha and his pack. The alpha were the Royal family and we at Clandestine were the pack. However, when they were all killed, the balance shifted. There was no pack leader, so chaos broke out, things started to fall apart and non-therians, or 'non-spirits' as we call them, noticed us. Things have gone from bad to worse as the number of rogues have kept increasing. We need a new leader but finding the right one is the issue!

"There are rumours that one Royal survived, and now there's a hunt to find him. We want to get him back on the throne so that balance can be restored once again before it's too late. It's a race against time that will decide all our fates. Can we live in peace or will there be the war of all wars that will not only destroy therians, but also all of humanity?" Her eyes stayed on me whilst she told me everything, and as hard as I tried to digest the information, I felt like I'd walked into a fantasy novel, and that made me burst into a fit of giggles which wasn't appreciated by River.

"Okay, that's a lot of information. I'm sorry I'm laughing but it's just sooooo unbelievable that my brain can't process half of what you've said. Let's say this is all true, and Clandestine is some undercover, secret, world-saving organization—why am I mixed up in it?" I had to bite my tongue hard to not laugh at the words which escaped my lips.

"You're one of us," she stated.

"Trust me, love. I'm no protector and I'm definitely not an actress. You have your wires crossed." I gestured down to my five-foot two-inch, average body. "I'm not built to be a fighting machine and I definitely haven't got hidden talents, unless you count eating as one."

"I know you're not an active member. Not yet, anyway. You never wanted to be, but you *are* one of us." She leaned in smirking and whispered, "You're a therianthrope!"

Tyler's POV

How did things turn out like this? I got to her in time to wrap my arms around her, praying that my body could withstand the impact. Making sure her head was tucked in, my spirit came out to shield us. I had no choice but to let it out even though it's forbidden to let any non-spirits see us in our therian forms. I couldn't brace the landing and we were thrown into the air. I tried but she still ended up with cuts and a couple of broken ribs. River has her sedated and Leo is flipping his switch. As usual, he wanted to play the hero!

****

Leaving her was a bad idea; I could hear her fear. Running from my shoot as fast as my legs could carry me, I threw myself into the air, allowing me enough time to change and land on the ground as my wolf. Speeding as the moonlight lit up my path, I arrived only to find Mina in her room with a rogue mutt at her feet. He had his mouth open and the thoughts running through his head triggered my wolf to take over. Mina always had this effect on me and my wolf, even before my spirit became a part of me. I recognised her as mine.

Chapter Three

"Am I meant to know what that is?" I whispered.

"It would have been helpful, yes. That way you would have understood everything the moment you got here, but thanks to someone's selfishness, we have to start over! Get changed, we'll go get some food, and once you're full I'll show you exactly what I mean. If you promise not to pass out."

Throwing clothes at me, she explained that there was a food court here on Clandestine grounds. The food was championed by world-renowned chefs and I had to taste it to believe it. River's impatience was familiar. As I pulled down the navy wool dress, I noticed a woman in the corner who gave me a fright at first. She stood silently watching us, covered completely from head to toe in a blue dress with a cloak. Her dark skin stood out against the light colouring of her garment and her eyes were adorned with a gold shimmer and thick black eyeliner. Her eyes were a deep brown and her uncoloured lips glistened. I was a little awestruck, I must admit. I had never laid eyes on a woman dressed like that before, but even more so, I had never seen a woman so beautifully graceful.

It oozed out of her.

River gestured towards her to come forward, and as the woman walked, everything seemed to be in slow motion.

She was almost floating as she walked.

"This is Caaliyah Skye, my dear friend; she watches over me." I smiled at her to acknowledge the introduction, but found myself gawking at her, but you'd have done the same. When she got closer, the light bounced off the highest points of her face, making her appear more surreal, her skin flawless.

"Hello…you have a weird look on your face," she smiled. Her voice matched her face; it was calm and soothing. "Hello… err…you're beautiful." That was all I could say, and both

Caaliyah and River laughed in unison. "She initially has that effect on people, but it wears off when you see her temper." Caaliyah scowled at first, then burst out laughing in agreement.

I didn't even get a glimpse of myself in the mirror before she shoved me out the door. It took more than a minute to get me, moving as I stood marvelling at the gorgeous corridors. The walls were covered in delicate, gold filigree designs and pillars divided different murals. It was as though I was walking through a museum that would befit the housing of the Elixir of Life, Pandora's Box and the gold of El Dorado. I followed her outside, my mouth open, admiring the glamorous architecture, and eventually found myself in the centre of a huge estate. The grounds were spectacular with multiple well-kept buildings and dividing gardens. River zigzagged through the passing people and buildings. I turned around just for a minute, curious as to where I had been cooped up, and my jaw hit the floor. Magnificent doesn't even come close to describing the castle in the clouds that my eyes had rested upon. "River, where exactly is this place?" I asked as we arrived at the entrance to what I could only assume was the food place. It was easily found; you just needed to follow the multiple layers of yummy food smells.

"The clue is in the name, Mina. It's called Clandestine Academy for a reason."

I could hear the buzz of chattering from outside.

"Listen, when we get in there, keep your head down, and if anyone asks questions, don't react. I will answer for you." I nodded. Now was not the time to argue, as the smell of food had made my tummy rumble. It was an empty vessel that urgently needed filling.

I vaguely felt the stares but carried on walking, with my head down, to the food stations. The vast array of dishes made my head spin. I settled for grilled pepper tuna steak with asparagus, poached eggs, radish and green salad with a light balsamic vinaigrette. Dessert was a stack of brownies with peanut butter ice cream and fresh strawberries. Putting a piece of the tuna steak in my mouth, I almost cried out as it melted away in my mouth. I could feel constant staring and whispers, as people had started to pay attention to us, and all I could do was eat. There was no way I was going to let anything distract me from my food. River pinched her nose up at me with every bite of tuna I took, so I could only assume that she didn't like fish. Glancing over at her plate, I saw a lot of colourful vegetables; I tried not to reciprocate the look I received. Caaliyah wasn't eating at all. She just stood behind River, watching everyone else, which seemed weird, but I didn't think to question it.

By the time I reached my dessert, the hall had quieted down and the focus on us had become outright rude. I wanted to say something sarcastic like: "Take a picture, it lasts longer." But I didn't want to garner more interest, so I just kept quiet, relishing each bite of my brownie. A guy walked over and stood at the side of our table. He was looking at River, but our eyes met a couple of times. His skin was a rich brown and he had thick black hair with matching brows. His dark eyes were lined with black and I had to admit he was extremely handsome. I guess Clandestine clearly had a type. A group of girls caught my attention. They were making such a dramatic fuss that, as a female, I felt slightly embarrassed. They were a little old to be part of a melodramatic fan club. I understood their enthusiasm as I could be the same with a select few dreamy people, but this was way beyond that.

I tried to ignore him, as River suggested, but she was completely unfazed. Last night had made me edgy.

"Hey River, what brings you out to us *common* folk, don't tell me it's the new meat? She doesn't seem that special." I watched River look up at him as she answered, but I decided not to pay attention. He could've just said, "Hi," and introduced himself, rather than making things uncomfortable, but I guess he'd left his manners at his table. He made sure the 'new meat' comment sounded somewhat condescending; we're a little too old for drama. "This is Mina, my best friend. I would be careful with that tone Cairo, you don't want unnecessary trouble, not with your father already playing favouritism games with Hameed... Mina, this is Cairo Yahyah."

"Who's Cairo?" I asked River my question, giving him back a little taste of his own medicine. He wasn't happy, but you reap what you sow.

"I'm Cairo, third in line for the throne of Egypt." Wait, what? A piece of brownie got caught in my throat, making me cough and splutter as River rushed around to tap by back. Did he just say throne? He's a prince? Well, now I know why he sounds so obnoxious; being a prince must have gotten to his head.

"Wow, do you start every conversation like that?" I sniggered unconsciously, it wasn't my best moment. "Well, Cairo, as you already know, I'm Mina. I'm not in line to any throne and I don't like conversing with people who think they're better than others."

He lowered himself, so he was at eye level with me, and looked directly into my eyes, smouldering. I guess that look had taken down many a girl, but I had to refrain from laughing. The moment was just wrong for that; he ruined the mood. River caught me teasingly wink at him and sprayed water everywhere. Cairo was cute, in the sun-kissed prince kinda way, but we got off on the wrong foot, and first impressions count.

I stood up out of my chair, trying to keep a smile plastered on my face. It was time to head back; this was enough of an excursion for the day.

"Excuse me, I need to get back." River started packing up our trays as she followed. I walked past Cairo, only to be forcefully grabbed by him.

"You need to learn to be nice when you're at the bottom of the food chain," he asserted, gritting his teeth for extra emphasis, his fingers digging into my arms. River dropped her tray and was immediately in Cairo's face, or should I say chest. I'm short but River is on an even smaller scale at four feet eleven.

"You better let go of that arm before you find my foot up your backside!" she demanded. There was a moment of chaos and Caaliyah had Cairo pinned against the wall face first. Cairo let go of my arm and as I rubbed it, he forced a smile and apologised to River.

"I'm sorry, River; you know I struggle with my temper, it's genetic. I think you need to teach her some manners or she'll get herself in a lot of bother. Can you get your pet off me now?"

What an absolute pig; first, he didn't even apologise to me, then he called Caaliyah a pet. I was about to put him straight, but my words caught in my mouth as River whacked Cairo right across the head so hard that people started jumping out of their seats and running towards us. This is not what I had signed up for.

Getting out of the hall as fast as my little legs could carry me, I questioned how I had kept my composure. Cairo tried to scare me because I had walked away from him. The guy obviously had issues. I could hear River shouting my name as she tried to catch up with me, but I kept on moving.

"You could at least slow down. I hate running. Cairo was a complete idiot and I'm sorry you had to go through that. It was mostly directed at me; we have history." Her tone was anxious.

"River, I hate confrontation, and the longer I'm here, the more I feel like I don't belong. I really want to go home." I had no idea how I found my way back to the room as my sense of direction was usually appalling.

"This *is* your home Mina. We've tried to give you all the space that was asked of us. However, we need you now more than ever, and I *know* you need us. You can only let your animal spirit lie dormant for so long before your body starts to shut down. Have you never asked yourself why you keep passing out? You're fighting against what makes you stronger and whole." River, who was babbling again, sat me in a chair in front of the bathroom door.

"I thought you said animal just then. Why didn't Caaliyah come with you?"

"I did say animal spirit…she'll be here." River was pacing now. I could tell she was agitated; who wouldn't be after what had just happened? She was half talking to me and half mumbling to herself. It was weird to watch. "Animal spirit? Okay, this is weird… I don't want to sound like a whiny child, but I'd like to go home." She held my hand as I stood up to leave.

"We need you, Mina. With your help, we can find the missing Royal. You were so close before and then the accident happened. Please don't leave. Let me prove to you that therianthropes exist. You say it sounds like fiction, but I can show you; just trust me." She led me into the bathroom and, putting the water on, stepped into the tub whilst removing her clothes. I was trying hard to figure out what she was doing, but it genuinely looked as though she was in the middle of some sort of a breakdown. She was muttering.

"Don't be scared; remember it's me." Scared of what? River started to make some gross snapping sounds and as I looked at her, I saw the pain in her face. Her body started to move in an odd non-human way. She squirmed and wriggled as she let out painful cries. I realised that the snapping sound was her body— her bones, to be precise. As her body writhed in pain, I thought I was going to be sick. I felt the bile rise in my mouth. I closed my eyes for a second and heard her cry out. I saw her golden skin change and a film of scales started to cover her body that turned into an iridescent blue-purple, like a snake. No. Not a snake, a fish?

I had to be hallucinating. Pinching myself, I winced. Nope, I couldn't do this. I just got up and ran as my head felt like it was about to implode. What had just happened? Things like this weren't real. Please let me be dreaming. I kept moving as fast as possible, trying to avoid a group of girls who moved along with me, blocking my way.

"I'm sorry, excuse me," I said looking up, only to be met with a forceful shove that almost landed me on my butt.

What was it with aggression in this place?

"She speaks. Do you know how long we've been waiting for you?" they all said in eerie harmony.

"Am I meant to know who you are?" This place and these people were starting to make me irritable.

"Know? You think showing Cairo up as *your* introduction to us all was a good idea?" said one of them as she moved to the front, standing between two other girls who looked just like her. These girls were Cairo's embarrassing groupies.

"He's a prince!" exclaimed another. No shit, Sherlock; I was there when he introduced himself.

"Look, I don't know what's going on, but what happened with Cairo was his fault." They all snapped their heads towards me like they were attached to each other. Then came the shrieking cackle, which no words can describe. I just stood there feeling my skin crawl. The five of them started to move towards me and the girl at the front raised her hand, striking my face. I was backed into a corner as they surrounded me, taking it in turns to slap me, laughing with every blow. I tried to defend myself but there was only so much I could do against five of them. I found myself on my knees, and then, suddenly, it all stopped. I slowly moved my arms away from shielding my face and watched them cower, taking a few steps back. They were fearful. Moving quickly all the while, their eyes were transfixed behind me. The trickles I could feel running down my face invaded my eyes. I tried wiping it, only to whimper from pain. I saw droplets fall to the ground; it was blood. And it was as the blood hit the ground that I was engulfed by the sweet smoky scent from last night, and a low rumble shook the floor beneath me. The girls started to scream as they ran away.

"Don't move," he said, and I turned to stone. I couldn't move. His scent was driving me crazy and all I wanted to do was to look at him.

"If you look at me and I see the cuts on your face, I'll have no choice but to tear 'em to shreds. So, don't turn around! Are you okay?" I heard him swear under his breath and could sense the clear warning of danger in his voice. I had no idea what was drawing me to him and fought the urge to look at him, feeling unable to control it.

"I said are you okay?" he repeated more aggressively.

"I'm okay…" my voice came out all raspy.

"Don't leave…stay where I can see you." I finally recognised his voice; he was the guy who had told River off. My curiosity gave way and I couldn't stop myself from looking over my shoulder. I was left with emptiness. Why did he disappear? I saw River running towards me with mascara-trailed tears running down her face. I stood up; the pain was no longer there.

"Mina, what happened? Why do you have blood on you? I'm sorry. I should have waited. It was too soon; you were trying to leave. I got desperate and couldn't think. So I just shifted; my spirit is a sea serpent." Unable to focus on River, I mentally concluded that I'd be staying at Clandestine.

River's POV

I missed her so much, even though I knew it's dangerous for Mina to be at Clandestine. I couldn't handle her not being here. After Dermarcos, it was Mina who kept me together. In my darkest times, she showed me light. For five years I felt suffocated. I was a recluse, doing nothing other than work. I never went out like I used to. Without her, a part of me was missing and now I was finally able to breathe. If only Leo had given her a choice before removing her memories, we wouldn't have needed to start over.

She needed to know that she was what holds us all together, especially Tyler. Without him and Leo, we may not make it out of this hell, and she knows how to stop those dumb brothers from killing each other. I love her more than my own self. She's the

32

baby sister I never had, and nothing will get in between me and her protection, not even Clandestine.

Chapter Four

Washing the blood off of my arms and face, my thoughts returned to Mr Smokey-Sweet. My heart hadn't settled, and I had this indescribable need to be with him. It hadn't even been that long since Jesse and I broke up, and here I was, fawning over some other guy. What about the fact that I hated physical contact? Why was this guy any different? Just having him near me made me feel complete, with an underlying desire that was so new to me.

I remembered a conversation I'd had with Clay, who said: "Everything happens for a reason, and at times we won't understand it, but trust me, there's a high probability that Jesse isn't the one for you. You just have to close that door so another one can open in its place." I teased him about it afterwards, asking if that was the reason why he was forever changing girlfriends. He tried to smack me and missed; I was pretty pleased with myself for dodging the contact in time. Recalling the conversation, it made sense. I think of Jesse a lot, but it's not the same. The dull ache had long gone.

Who was this guy and why did he set off the butterflies in my stomach by just being present? I can't explain the frustration of wanting to see him; my imagination is building up an image of him that is probably too good to be true and I don't want that.

At times like this, I needed Clay. He kept me focused, always providing the reality check that I needed. He kept the crazy at a minimum, and more than anything, was the familiar face I needed right now—a part of home, a part of me before this.

Taking my phone out, I messaged him, just to let him know that I was okay. Even though he knew I was safe, he hadn't heard it from me.

"I'm okay, I miss you." I decided to leave out all the crazy stuff that had been happening to me since I'd got here.

I didn't need him to be caught up in this, playing the hero.

Looking in the mirror, I recoiled; dark circles surrounded my eyes and my skin was in bad shape. It was looking pale and unhealthy in comparison to my usual golden complexion.

"Mina, are you okay in there?" asked River; she sounded worried. I opened the door to let her in.

"I'm okay, just shocked. It's a lot to digest all at once, and the people here are mean; first Cairo, then those girls. I really don't like it." It scared me that people could act that way.

"I understand. Trust me it wasn't like this before; that's why we need to find the Royal; you were close to them. There's a power struggle, a hierarchy system, and people at the top think they have a right to mistreat those they deem beneath them, like Angel Pierce and her 'clique'. They believe they can treat you how they like because you're not connected with your spirit animal, which is wrong, but it's happening more often than before. They aren't the only ones either. There are a lot more who believe they can do what they like to those they see as being beneath them, especially the guttersnipes. Those guys are treated so bad, and it's not fair."

"Guttersnipes?" It was a weird thing to call people.

"Guttersnipes are therianthropes who have mixed blood, partly of a therianthrope and partly a shadow. They don't fit in either role properly, so they're the lowest in the hierarchy and are usually seen as being unnatural. We tend to stay away from them, unfortunately."

"What's a shadow?" I was intrigued, and let's face it, it couldn't get any weirder than a shape-shifting performing arts school, which fronted as a black ops organisation saving the world. Right?

"A shadow is the equivalent of a bodyguard. They are committed to one therianthrope. It's basically like a blood connection and they stick to them until either one dies. A shadow chooses the therian they protect and they all have a unique power. They're known for being able to manipulate the elements. However, it's said that some of them have even teleported; only the therian knows the true powers of their shadow. Take Leo's shadow for example; she could remove any specific memory links. They also have a hierarchical system in their groups; the ones at the top usually protect the elite. You'll learn all this one step at a time.

"One other thing is that the relationship between a shadow and their therianthrope is unique. They are so intertwined with each other, they create their own bubble which gets complicated when mates are involved. Shadows don't have a mate, so most of the times they fall in love with their therian counterparts. Occasionally, those feelings are reciprocated, and they have a child, therefore creating a 'Guttersnipe', one who is neither a therian nor shadow. You met Caaliyah; she is my shadow."

Now it makes sense why Caaliyah just hovers around River, but how backwards was this concept that you had to be careful about who you fell in love with? I could swear I had just walked into an alternate universe, still living in the 18th century. I didn't know whether to laugh or cry.

"So where do I fit in, do I have a shadow? And by mate, do you mean a partner? Are you and Caaliyah a thing? And how come I am only just finding out about this?" I found myself wondering if I have a shadow, and what about a mate?

"You're a therian; we don't know what your spirit animal is. Seven years ago, you had to leave us. You were with an indigenous group of people who were helping you to control your spirit. It was really hard for you to change. Most therianthropes get their strength from their animal form but you took out both Tyler and Leo in your human form. We knew then we had to keep you hidden, especially after the Royals were killed, and with your strength, we think you can protect the last .one. The rogues didn't want anyone to stand up for the right thing as they want to overthrow the therian kingdom. They don't think a Royal family is what the people need as it's seen as soft and therianthropes are meant to be fierce, a step above humans."

A step above humans? Are they serious? I scoffed; anyone who thinks they're better than the next person…they had some serious problems. River carried on in her animated way and I saw Caaliyah creep back in behind her. "A few people thought you were the last Royal, but Leo laughed it off. He would've known, seeing as he thinks he's your mate. He would've been able to 'feel' it, but he never got the chance to mark you before your so-called 'accident', and even though it drove him crazy, he had his shadow wipe your memory of anything to do with therianthropes and left you with Tyler. Your abilities have been dormant. That's why you've kept passing out; you need a trigger to help you change. Leo made it look like you died in the accident. He did what was necessary to keep you alive, because that attack on you was intentional." I thought I was in an accident caused by my parents.

"Who's Leo?" There are a lot of men in my life that I didn't even know about.

"Leo Kang, he's the best defence soldier in the legion, ruthless in battle and doesn't see anything but the end goal. The one thing that he and his brother have in common is that they are both merciless fighters who protect anything or anyone they see as theirs. Tyler could definitely give him a run for his money on the same grounds. You'd wish death came at you faster if they caught you harming anyone in their circle. They are both respected in the field, Leo as the soldier and Tyler as the hunter. They're more alike each other than they would care to admit.

"We all fear the Kang brothers. Everyone avoids Leo at all costs, as he's just grumpy all the time. Everyone wants to befriend Tyler, even though he's cold. Once you're in his circle, you're protected by him; he would die for you. Leo is crazy; he can rip any therianthrope to shreds and doesn't need much to set him off. He was cruel even towards Tyler who's his half-brother; same dad, different mum. He hated the idea of mixing bloodlines. He was brought up on that concept and then, suddenly, his dad changed his mind. What's worse is his father mated with a woman who had a wolf spirit, or as Leo taunts, 'a mutt'. For him, mating with a non-spirit was better than mixing therian blood to create hybrids.

"That was until he met you. You calmed Leo and gave him a different perspective on life and people. You were different— warm, bubbly and didn't take any of his macho nonsense. I think that's how he got his soft spot for you. All women feared him, and you just smacked him; from what I can recall you called him a sexist pig right after. You helped bond the brothers, well… you helped them to be in one room for longer than a minute and not kill each other. Tyler did everything you said, even if he hated it. You two were joined at the hip from a young age; he followed you around like a lost pup. Leo, minus the temper, has a good head for battle and great leadership skills which was perfect as he was part of the Royal circle and now he's in line for the throne. You made Leo accept me too; we're like a dysfunctional family." River laughed to herself.

"Without you, Leo changed. He picked fights just to blank you out and became so hostile. Tyler tried stopping him but that bond broke with you leaving, and they blamed each other for what happened to you. Tyler knew where you were and wouldn't tell anyone. The fights I had to break up, it gives me shivers just thinking about it. No one can put either of them down in a fight. Leo's spirit is a lion for crying out loud. He's like the ultimate fighting machine, and not just any lion. He's basically a descendent of the *nemeon* spirit. Tyler's spirit is a combination of a lion and a wolf; now let that sink in. Tyler didn't want to bring you back because you were safe out of it, but because we, the therians, need Leo to lead and take the throne. He caved in as he was aware that only you can give his brother focus. They were both hurting bad. I was too; I needed my best friend."

She was hugging me by the end of her history update.

"With you by our side, we could find the last remaining Royal. If you can get the brother's back on 'not killing each other' terms, we have a fighting chance," she explained.

"So, about Tyler? You said we've been friends since we were children?" I wondered if either of them was my mystery man.

"Tyler is different to Leo; you two butt heads a lot. He teases you and you flip out at him; it's amusing to watch. It's plain to see you have a strong bond, even though you keep saying you're friends to everyone else. I see how he looks at you and I saw how you looked at him too. That gets on Leo's nerves the most, your relationship with Tyler. Leo can't stand the fact that you met his brother first and you're close to him. You and I have had this conversation before; you can never give Tyler up on your own. Or should I say, you never would have given him up, as he was part of you," she said with a smile.

"When do I get to meet them?" I was curious.

"Leo is around all the time. Now he's with the Royal circle. They're 'the council' who want Leo to take the throne; they think he's easy to manipulate. Some of them have egos they can barely carry, acting all righteous when it's more about power and control for them. Be careful. I'm sure you'll meet them soon.

He'll be here tonight to officially reintroduce himself to you. Tyler is out on some assignment, apparently a group of rogues have been causing havoc somewhere in Korea and it's helpful that he's part of an idol group over there.

"Anyway, enough catch up; I need to get you to the CEO's office so that you can get your schedule like the rest of the newbies. This, by the way, is your room; mine is just across from you. We have the East wing and the guys have the West, apart from Tyler—he's secretly taken the room next to mine. Everything in between is training grounds, tutor rooms and the library. Let's go." She smiled and started skipping down the corridor, beckoning me to follow suit. That was never going to happen, obviously. Caaliyah walked with me.

"I'm glad you're back, Mina. River wasn't the same without you. She hides her pain well. Things are looking up again. If you ever need anything, don't hesitate to ask. Any family of River's is my family too."

Her words were sweet, and I didn't think that River was someone who couldn't cope.

We arrived at an open space with about seventy other people who all hushed when we entered. There was a huge door with the same filigree design, but it had golden cogs all the way down. Taking the stairs was too much for my little legs, so I had to go for the lift option to arrive at our destination. I was practically panting a third of the way up, a reminder that I needed to work on my fitness and healthy lifestyle 'New Year's resolution' that I hadn't even dented yet, and it was almost autumn. It says a lot for someone who's had the same resolution for five years in a row. River knocked quiet loudly and the cogs started to move as if by magic.

I was met by the warmest chocolate eyes. They belonged to a handsome man, not much older than fifty. He had soft wrinkles around his eyes and mouth. He was in a suit with a cape on top. It was an actual cape, not the superhero kind, and looked more like a robe. I tried to not to reference any wizard comments, but I looked over at River, who gave me a knowing reply by rolling her eyes and miming for me to keep my mouth zipped. Well, I guess not everyone is a fan of magic. My comment was swallowed even before it came out.

"Miss Castillo, Miss Michaels, this has been a long time coming. Welcome home!" He nodded at River and then wrapped his arms around me in a bear hug. I tried not to squirm at the contact. He didn't even acknowledge Caaliyah, who was standing with us.

"You don't know how happy I am to see you here again. I didn't know if they would find you. I was so very hurt when you disappeared. When the late King brought you here with the others, I said I would take care of you all, but I failed him. Thank you for this second chance; I can finally repay my old friend."

The guy must've been close to the King as he seemed genuinely upset. I can't imagine the loss of a friend like that. I can't even think about anything happening to Clay without feeling physically sick.

"I'm sorry for your loss; there is a lot of information I need to digest. I still don't understand how Clandestine works or what is expected of me. Mr…" Erm, I didn't even know who he was.

"Sorry, my name is Nathaniel Burozk. I run Clandestine Academy, the arts only. The combat side is for the Royal circle and the chargé d'affaires. Anyway, Miss Michaels, I have a letter that has been waiting for you. It's from the late King."

A letter for me, from a King?

"Please, call me Mina," I said as he unlocked a drawer in his desk and handed me an old envelope. There was a golden wax seal on it. I could hardly tell what the design was, but it had a crescent moon intertwining two letters, a W and an M.

"Unfortunately, we need to keep the formalities. After all, I will be your boss at Clandestine and I cannot give you preferential treatment, regardless of our previous ties. You will do as all the new recruits do, Miss Michaels." I didn't even try to respond, I was too busy reading the letter. I had a letter from actual royalty, me!

My little moon,

I guess I am no longer there to guide you; don't forget you are a strong young woman. Do not blame yourself for the way things have turned out. You weren't to know that death was coming for us all, but do not worry. I am with all my children in a better place and will wait for those who shall follow.

I hope Tyler is protecting you as he has done all these years, so that you can support Leo in taking over the throne. Keep him steadfast in being a just and kind leader.

Stay safe my sweet moon,

Your dearest friend,
William.

Nathaniel's POV

Mina looks a lot different to when she was a child and a teen. She has grown up more reserved and shy. It seems she has lost the spirit she once had, and we need that spirit. She can lead the way to the Royal. If William could entrust anyone with the truth, it would be this woman in front of me.

As hard as it is to understand the bond there was between her and the late King, she was special, not just to him but also to his children and his wife. They all doted on her, and I need her if we are to find the last Royal. She must lead the way.

Chapter Five

I could feel the eyes of both River and Nathaniel fixed on me, and I quickly brushed away the tears that had escaped mine. Why am I crying over a note? Why did it make my heart ache? What could have possibly been the bond between me and the Royal family? I was a nobody.

Nathaniel tried to glimpse the words on the letter, which was rude, and I cleared my throat as I watched him. He smiled weakly and just brushed his cape-robe before walking towards a printer, which looked odd and out of place in his office. Everything was antique or old, whichever way you want to put it. The only things that didn't fit the theme were the printer, desktop and a mobile phone hidden under some files next to a vintage dial out.

The room itself was dark with mahogany furnishings and lamps in odd places. One was on the bookshelf, another on the windowsill and a third by the door. There was also a chandelier dangling from the ceiling and a wall dedicated to a photomap, where dozens of photos hung. All of them included Nathaniel and someone else. I strained my eyes to get a better look, and to my surprise, I saw a few famous faces, which made me jump out of my seat. I saw a couple of my favourite actors, some who I'd had a crush on for years. It was difficult to contain my excitement until River pulled me back into my seat, shushing me.

"Miss Michaels, this is your schedule. The sessions repeat till you graduate the class. It is difficult at first but keep at it; we can't have you falling behind. You're already in classes with students that are much younger. Do not make a show of yourself or Clandestine—work hard. I will be looking at your tutor's notes, and if needed, I will rework your schedule and fit in more sessions. I don't allow tardiness whoever you may be." He seemed a lot blunter than when I first walked in; he obviously took this arts business oh so seriously.

I took the sheet out of his hand and my jaw dropped when I saw the list.

8:00 am – Breakfast

9:00 am – Languages, History and Culture Studies.

11:00 am – World Art, Music and Dance, Theatre and Performance.

1:00 pm – Lunch

2:00 pm – Etiquette and Common Manners.

4:00 pm – Defence and Resistance Training.

6:00 pm – Meditation, Spirit Unification and Chi.

8:00 pm – Supper

"This isn't what I expected, and I very much doubt I can do, much of what is here. I'm sorry, I can stay and help out in any way I can, but I can't do any of this." Seriously dance and theatre? Defence and Resistance? Spirit unification? They don't even go hand in hand.

"You cannot stay at Clandestine if you do not train to achieve the set goals. Everyone who is a therian goes through this. If you do not want to stay, Miss Michaels, that is fine. The gates are open, but like I said, no preferential treatment is given to anyone."

He seemed offended and I didn't want to make a scene. River looked nervous and I read her signals well enough to just accept defeat. I had to stay here, that much I knew, grit my teeth for a few weeks, till I understand where I fitted in and then figure out if I am what they say I am.

"I will try my best," I smiled half-heartedly.

"We don't try here. We do. You start immediately. I will, however, allow you some time to see your family." With that, he briskly showed us out of his door and another guy entered as we were leaving. Everyone in the waiting area still looked nervous, so I guess I was in the same boat as a lot of them. There was one guy in the corner surrounded by female admirers. He cheekily winked as our eyes met, only to receive an automatic eyeroll from me.

"Rude much?" I asked as the door closed behind us.

"That's just his way; don't take it to heart. Nathaniel has always been stern, but he has a warm heart. He wants the best for us all. He worked hard to put Clandestine on the map as an all-round arts company. We're successful because of the tight ship he runs. This is more than just a cover or a business, it's his life's work." I couldn't help but roll my eyes even though I understood when I saw all the successes pinned to his wall. As we were finishing our conversation, I saw a few of the seated people make a line for us. This was a little intimidating after what had happened earlier but they all had eager smiles, so I felt more welcomed. One of the boys came up to us. He had long hair and a strong physique; his eyes were on River.

"Hi, my name is Hahona, do you mind if I get a picture?" River blushed as I looked on in confusion; why did he want her photo?

"Yes, sure, is here okay?" she replied coyly.

This started a chain reaction and so many of them came up for pictures. A pretty girl called Emilia Rose asked me to take a picture of them both. I heard her tell River how inspirational her body activism was.

"What is going on?" I asked as we were crowded.

"I forgot to mention, I'm a model." After blocking them all, Caaliyah ushered us to the lift.

"Honestly though, this schedule is something else. How likely is it that I will even survive the first week?" I asked.

"Not very. I was in bed unable to move every night and I did nothing but sleep at the weekends, but you have us. We'll get you through it." This was not the answer I wanted, but I calmed my inner tantrum as we made it back to my room. I pinned the schedule to the back of my door as a reminder of what was to come.

"So, I better get used to this place. River can you help me pack and come home with me? I need some familiarity. I mean, not only am I a 'therian' but I have to go back to 'school' surrounded by mean girls and people who apparently want to kill me." Yup, life is full of surprises, whether you like it or not.

"Seriously, you need to stop with the finger quotations, it's annoying. Look, all you need to know is you're one of us, and we will keep you safe."

"You should get ready for tonight; Leo's going to be coming over. Unless you're going for the sickly look?"

"Ha, you're funny," I said, throwing a cushion. "Help me!" I pleaded. It had to be the guy from my room last night and out in the corridor today. Leo was the one who'd been saving me. River said he believes he's my mate. It took over an hour to get me ready. I don't know why waxing everything was necessary. I can barely feel my skin, but being dark haired and light skinned, doesn't help. No one wants to see a female with peach fuzz above her lips, apparently. River had me in a long wine maxi with a slit down one side, showing way too much skin for my liking. She straightened out my candy floss hair till it was silky to the touch and fell down my shoulders. My makeup was light with coverage only where necessary, like my dark circles and a few breakout scars, with full lashes, nude lips and blush. She filled in my thick brows and gave them definition. I couldn't remember the last time I looked this pretty. I tried not to cover my face much, as my skin needs to breathe. I struggle with hormonal breakouts, another thing to add to the joys of being female. Why not make the girl a pimple patch when she's already stressing over her monthly bleeding? Like seriously.

"Okay, I'm off," River said, walking towards the door.

"Off where? You can't leave me alone," I replied, rushing to hold onto her.

"Trust me, I don't want to be here when you two start to reacquaint yourselves with each other," she laughed.

"Ciao, don't break anything," she gave me a kiss and winked.

Walking around the room, I heard the knock first. It stopped me in my tracks and I just stood looking at the door as it opened. As soon as the corridor light filled my dimly lit room, I changed my mind and stared at the floor. His scent filled the room. It was not as smoky as the previous times, but rather musky, and there weren't any sweet notes. Did I imagine the sweetness before? I could feel it pushing against my senses. I slowly looked up and a guy dressed in black walked in and stood in front of the door. He had on some snug fit jeans tucked into black leather lace-up boots, a loose sweatshirt and a wool trench. His jawline was dusted with dark stubble that matched his thick hair, which fell over his eyes, and he was wet from the rain, I assumed. His lips were a light pink shade, equally balanced and his sharp nose fitted perfectly on his face. He wasn't as big as I imagined, like a lion, but well defined with a medium build. He seemed to be taking me in from the feet up, and then our eyes met. His eyes slanted a little—light and stark against his black hair. He was striking to say the least, like no one I'd ever seen before, and trust me I've seen some good-looking guys in my time. Take Clay, for example, or the few actors that I fangirl over, but Leo was on a different level. I had felt good about how I looked a few minutes ago but now realised that I'm plain in comparison. What was this guy thinking? Is he sure I'm his mate? "Leo?" I asked, smiling, only to be met with a deep growl that made me jump. His eyes kept me captive as he marched towards me, not taking his eyes off mine. I literally couldn't move.

Leo's POV

Seeing her standing there under the dim lights reignited the burning desire within me. Mina had been the first girl to take control of my every emotion. She made me feel anger, sadness, pain, love, you name it, I felt it. She appealed to my lion. Her soft rose scent tamed the beast, who craved the moment I would make her mine. I'm hoping it's a choice that she makes before seeing my unlawful brother again. There is nothing I wouldn't do to have her. Tonight, I'll let my spirit draw on hers, there is no way she is equipped to fight off his presence, not when she hasn't learnt how to draw power from hers. She'll be mine without even knowing. It's been too long, and my heart still belongs to her. She has to be mine. As our eyes met I felt my beast come forward with a growl, ready to take what was before us as his.

Chapter Six

There was no hello. He had me in his arms immediately, backing me up towards the wall, and even though I wanted to push him off for being in my personal space, I couldn't bring myself to move him for some reason. He was too close for comfort; my body wasn't doing what my brain was screaming at it to do and everything just felt a little off. My arms reached up to entwine my fingers in his hair and pull him closer. I was on my tiptoes and it was a struggle trying to balance. What was going on? Why could I not control this situation? My mind was becoming cloudy and blurred but I didn't feel scared, more annoyed. I wanted to punch Leo's lights out but physically couldn't do it.

He lifted me off the ground, wrapping my legs around his waist. His nose was nuzzled into my neck, and as he inhaled he let out another growl, low and intimate, which had me pulling him closer.

I don't know how or when, but we ended up on a chair. My fingers in his hair and his hands travelling down my back, escalating his breathing. I kept telling myself to stop what was happening, but I couldn't help it. My body was working against me, and in that moment, everything changed. I inexplicably needed him and that was it. My entire focus was on him; I didn't know if I could keep it together. Just on cue, he pulled my head towards him to plant a soft kiss on the hollow of my neck, making me quiver. He followed with a trail up to my lips, only to pause inches away, before edging slowly closer. He hovered his lips close to mine, allowing me to feel his deep breaths against them. Unconsciously, I licked my lips and leaned towards him, my hands pressed against his solid chest for support. I touched my lips against his, and in a matter of seconds, he deepened the kiss.

With every lingering minute, the kiss became more urgent. I pulled us apart, needing to catch my breath. He allowed me seconds before pulling me closer to him and kissing me again, whispering: "I'm not apologising for my need of you; I've waited far too long." He growled deeply from his belly and I felt the rumble beneath my legs as he crashed his lips against mine and drew my body closer.

I had to tear myself from his iron grip as my need for oxygen was greater. This could be a long night. How can a guy kiss without breathing? I felt as though I had been on a thirty-minute run. As I tried to catch my breath, he just held me. I had his forehead against my chin. It was an out-of-body experience, and just as it started to dawn on me that I had just made out with a stranger, without being in control of the situation, I could feel the bile rise in my mouth.

"Mina, I missed you," he whispered. I tried to reply, but as I opened my mouth, I vomited.

"Shoot! Mina, are you okay?!" The concern in his voice was real. In a split second, he had me in the bathroom, holding my hair back as I threw up into the toilet. Not exactly the demure, ladylike look I was going for, but maybe it would make him think twice before he kissed me again. After I'd finished emptying my stomach, he took my face into his hands and planted me with gentle kisses. Doesn't vomit breath put this guy off? Eww!

There was a niggling feeling in the pit of my stomach that I couldn't put my finger on as he carried me bride style back into my room and placed me in the seat that we were previously in. He then took off his coat and vomit covered shirt and sat on the floor by my leg. My eyes fleeted across his well-formed muscles, the dim lights reflected every part of his bare chest and I struggled to stay seated. As I relaxed back into the chair, I felt his arm on my leg which was a weird picture to look at, a grown man stroking my leg. I stifled a laugh when I thought that it could be a cat thing?

We spent a bit of the evening in silence. I had questions, but right now, I needed to figure out what had just happened and bizarrely, I felt his needs. It was as though he was projecting them on to me. Leo just wanted me there, no ill intention. I could sense what he was feeling, so without thinking, I got onto the floor next to him and he pulled me into his lap. His grip tightened around my waist as he pulled me in closer to him and rested his face on my back. In that moment, he was utterly childlike. He didn't seem to be what River had described him as—a ruthless and formidable soldier.

He frequently kissed my shoulder and there was that overpowering feeling again; in a situation where I would normally flinch, I was grounded. It was an inner battle that I could physically feel. Leo was making me act like I never had done before. Why don't I feel disgusted every time he held me? On the other hand, I did puke my guts out when he kissed me. Was that a lack of oxygen or something else?

This guy made me feel so sure of myself. I mean I looked plain in comparison and he just kissed me after I threw up; could he really love me? I felt something towards Leo, but it wasn't love. Whatever it was, I knew its overlay was complete, utter, uncontrollable lust. I tried not to move despite the numbness that grew in my legs, but to no avail. The cramping had started, and as I tried to readjust myself and stop crying out from laughter due to the pins and needles, Leo let out a growl that was crossed with a groan. He pushed me to the ground, jumped up and took two steps back.

"What the hell, why did you do that?" It hurt; he could've just put me down gently or given me some sort of warning.

"Trust me, you don't want to be near me right now, unless you want to end up over there," he nodded towards the bed, raising an eyebrow and making me blush profusely.

"Err…no, it's cool," I said, while avoiding his eyes and dusting myself off. Reaching up I touched my cheeks that had exploded with heat and I could hear him chuckle.

"What's so funny?" I asked scowling at him.

"I've missed your innocent reactions, it seems you're still the same even after so many years. I thought things would have changed with you having a boyfriend," he said, smirking as he walked towards me.

"Ex-boyfriend… It wasn't right for me, I wasn't ready." He was standing in front of me still smirking, which was annoying. Why was I even explaining?

"Good, cos I don't like anyone touching what's mine," he whispered, sending chills up my spine.

"I'm not anyone's!" Struggling with what's right and what my body was telling me was tiring me out.

"Are you sure?" he asked, placing kisses along my collarbone, making me swallow whatever sarcastic reply was about to come out of my mouth.

"Leo?" He raised his eyes to meet mine, which made me unintentionally gulp. *I must snap out of this mood*, I thought, shaking my head to focus my mind.

"I need answers." Taking a step back, he lifted me up again on to his lap and we resumed sitting.

"Are you sure this is safe?" I asked, laughing.

"Yes, but no sudden movements," he said, winking.

"First, do you know what my spirit animal is?" I asked him.

"I know you're like a nemeon," he flashed a confident smile.

"I don't know what you are. Every time you tried to shift it hurt you to the point of passing out. You needed to get stronger mentally and physically first, so you went to this private retreat. The king had you escorted secretly," he said, kissing my hand.

"Are you saying I'm fat?" I know it's off topic, but he said I needed to be physically stronger.

"No, you're not fat, I didn't even say that. Not every therianthrope can physically shift because the pain is unbearable. It's never been necessary to take our animal forms; we just draw power from them to be a better version of ourselves. With every shift, your bones break to create the new structure, so it takes a lot out of us. But you're beautiful in the moments before you pass out. There's this ethereal glow I've never seen before. You're strong enough to have me on my back," he said laughing, whilst stroking my arm.

"So you're saying I can kick your butt?" I was intrigued.

"No, I just let you." He kissed my cheek.

"Uh huh, sure. So why did you let me go?" My question stopped him in his tracks and his look of torment made me want to take it back.

"You would have died if you were by my side. I wouldn't have been able to live if anything had happened to you. I've always been a loner, I liked it that way. Nothing to tie me down or make me lose focus. I didn't let women get near me; I just didn't see them. I didn't see you coming. My goal was to protect the Royals and I failed at that. I couldn't protect them, even though it was my duty and there was no way I was going to lose you. The king wanted us to protect you too and I was not going to fail at that." He was shuddering by the end. I reached up and pulled him closer.

"It's not your fault; it was out of your control. I'm still here and nothing will happen to me," I said, resting against his jaw. He pulled me closer.

"Do you know why I was close to the Royal family?" It was a question I needed the answer to.

"You and the King had a love for literature. You would read to each other. When you were fifteen, you interrupted a strategy meeting I was in with the King and the three Princes. You were in the library above his office; we didn't know you were there. We couldn't answer the question of how we could disarm a group with minimal damage to life. That was the King's way, he wanted to save rather than destroy and that put them all in danger. It was his blind faith in the goodness of all people. You showed us a way to draw out the rogues by using a decoy method and it worked. We didn't see that before, and that's why we needed a new set of eyes. You became a larger part and the Princes took to you too." Ha-ha, I couldn't even strategise my way out of a bad relationship and to think I used to advise soldiers going into battle.

"Why were the Royals killed?" I asked, wanting to understand.

"The King was a good man, he wanted us to all live in peace with each other, but like with all world politics, there were always groups whose thirst for power created hate and fuelled fear. These groups care for nothing, they have no rules, no faith and no compassion, so they kill everything and everyone in their path. Their goal is to create chaos, to feed off fear and make us all kill each other, therians and non-spirits alike. They want to set the world on fire and watch it burn. The King tried to stop all that; he and his family wanted to rule a people who had free will, who enjoyed being part of this community. We all have differences, whether it is communities of shadows, therians or non-spirits. They believed there's goodness even in evil people and that was essentially what got them killed."

How could seeing the good in people and a better life for all people become a death sentence? I didn't want to live to see the day where looking for the goodness in others was no longer an option.

"Is it true, you're going to be the next King?"

He paused a while, deep in thought. "Mina, my true place is at the side of a king; I've always been the right-hand man. I don't see myself as a king but until the last Royal is found and is ready to take the throne I have to play this part, it's what I owe the late King, my friend. I need to place his last heir, his blood on the throne or die trying." Determination ran through his voice. I'd like to help him and repay the kindness that was bestowed on me by the Royals.

"Do you know who the Royal is? Why isn't he ready?"

"I don't, but I'm sure my stupid brother does. He grew up in the Royal grounds and I've tried getting it out of him, even tried to beat it out of him. Tyler is defiant, he doesn't give things up easily, no matter the cost. I promised the late King I would protect the last Royal until it's time to reveal that an heir is still alive. There are therians and rogues alike still looking to wipe .out that bloodline completely and I can't push Tyler to reveal him, not yet anyway.

"The Royal bloodline keeps us thriving; it provides us with an opportunity to live a normal life if we want to. Being part of this world is a choice, so many therians choose to live dormant with non-spirits and it works for them. The rogues want to eradicate those who aren't honoured to be what we are; they see as traitors those who choose to live as non-spirits. This isn't an easy task, the world is basically being overrun by lunatics thinking they're better than everyone else, how can anyone manage that and bring order?"

"Why did you wipe my memories, and can you get your shadow to restore them please?" I asked, trying to change the direction of this grim conversation.

"It was the only way to keep you away from us, keep you safe. My shadow Clarissa is dead."

Way to go, Mina. I was trying to stray away from gloomy conversations.

"I'm so sorry for your loss, that must've been hard." I let the silence linger before asking my next question.

"Why couldn't you just tell me to leave instead of removing a big chunk of my life?"

"I didn't remove a big chunk, it was just the parts that were linked to all things therianthrope. If I'd told you to leave, you wouldn't have."

"What do you mean I wouldn't? I'm sure I could have if you asked."

"Being away from your mate can destroy a therian or damage them in ways that will change them forever. I didn't want to hurt you, wiping your memory was the only choice."

"You think…I'm your mate? Just off what you've just said, how did you get through it?" He shifted position and loosened his grip, he was keeping something from me.

"It was hard, but I focused on my work, plus I hadn't marked you, so our connection wasn't complete." He kissed my shoulder gently and I felt his lips linger. I could feel him trying to remove my doubts, but it wasn't working.

"Why are we mates, Leo?" I don't really know why I asked that question.

I turned to look at him, and from his expression of perplexity, he definitely wasn't expecting that question. "You saved me! Your heart, your love for all people therians and non-spirits alike, everything about you made me want to be a better person. I needed to create a better world for you. I've never thought of or cared for anyone before. You make me think twice and question things. You make me human." He smiled and kissed my head. "When you first touched me, you were rushing around Clandestine with papers in your hand and walked right into me. It was just before I met you in the library. That was the first time I felt a spark in my heart. To be honest, it was more like a jolt, a wake-up call, and when I looked at you, something happened. I wanted to kiss you and my animal growled, which scared you, making you flinch. The fear in your eyes made me want to protect you, so you filled my thoughts to the point where I couldn't concentrate, and I needed to be around you. When I found out you were only fifteen, it didn't change my feelings. I wouldn't hurt you in any way ever. I waited, we became friends and I fell for you further. I haven't looked back since. I love you!" He whispered this matter-of-factly whilst kissing the tip of my nose.

"How old are you?" He'd thought I was older when we first met, but he didn't look much older than me.

"I'm thirty-three." My mouth dropped.

"You're eight years older than me. When I was fifteen you were twenty-three, eww. That's a little bit weird." I tried not to feel creeped out, or show that I was, but it was too late.

"I never touched you or tried to; it wasn't like that!" He was hurt.

"I didn't mean it like that; it's just weird."

"Mina, I loved you for who you were, not for what I could take from you. If you don't love me, I would never do anything to destroy what we have." I believed him as everything from his eyes to his face was sincere.

My questioning stopped as he wanted to know more about me and what he had missed over the last few years. So, I talked about my job, my parents, Clay, which made him growl, and explained that we'd never been in a relationship. We were just close friends. When the topic of Jesse came up, he was constantly angry and kept cursing under his breath, even though I could hear every word.

The night passed with us just talking and catching up, as he constantly cuddled and kissed me. "Making up for lost time," he said when I asked him to stop. I must've drifted off, as I woke up with the blanket around me and the sun seeping through the curtains, its warmth kissing the front of my legs. Leo must have put me to bed before he left. Shifting to get comfortable, I knocked into something, and turned around to see Leo sleeping next to me shirtless. Holy cow, what happened last night? Freaking out, I looked down my body, sighing with relief that I had a long t-shirt and shorts on. I almost had a heart attack.

"Nothing happened, go back to sleep," he whispered, pulling me in and kissing the back of my head.

Tyler's POV

I knew Leo would try to get to her; we made a pact that we would let Mina decide which one of us was right for her. I've known since we were kids that Mina is the only focus in my life; without her, nothing makes sense to me.

From the moment I laid eyes on her as a child, my whole world shifted.

I left after speaking to the King, he asked me to protect her, and the only way to do that was to shift before she did. I was younger, so I didn't have time on my side, and Mina was already starting at fifteen. She was showing early signs. Women shift at eighteen, but her spirit was too strong to contain. The King knew that, so I had to leave and purposefully shift, forcing my bones to break earlier. Nothing but coming back to Mina kept me going. She met Leo when I left, and he selfishly released his lion spirit around her, so it would bring her spirit animal to the surface, even though she wasn't ready. Leo purposefully brought her to heat and dozens of therians tried to get at her, scaring her to the point of a breakdown. Her father kept her in a bubble, wanting her to connect to her spirit before she looked for a mate.

But that selfish pig was afraid that she would choose me as her rightful mate and drew out her spirit before she was ready, making her suffer. She constantly collapsed, always crying out in pain. She couldn't balance both her human self and animal counterpart.

Now he's with her, filling her with God knows what stories to occupy her mind and using his nemeon spirit to draw her in. It's taking everything from me to not force myself in there and rip her away from him, but I wouldn't be able to stop myself from hurting her in the process.

Chapter Seven

"I've got you, don't worry."

His piercing red eyes branded my soul as he choked and spluttered blood all over me, before leaping backwards over the edge, with me tucked in his arms...

He turned as we fell, placing me on top. Looking up at him, I realised this was the last face I'd see, everything but his eyes looked hazy.

"Mina, relax your body," he said, speaking a bit too calmly. I didn't even see his lips move.

His eyes told me everything his lips wouldn't say, the torment in them was a goodbye. He was going to break my fall because he trusted I'd make it.

"You can't leave me." Tears welled in my eyes and all I could do was let them fall.

"I'll never leave you, I'll always be there beside you, no matter where you are." He pulled me in closer as he let out a loud earth-shattering growl. Beneath my fingers, I felt him change. Thick black fur filled the spaces between my fingers as he grew taller, broader. Beneath his fur, I felt his muscular shape take form. He let out another howl of anguish.

The impact shook me. I felt my body fly up with his arms around my waist, pulling me back down onto his lifeless form. Ignoring the pain that seared through my body, I looked up to see his black fur dissolve from him and his face. The one I always see, still out-of-focus. I heard his howl echoing, ringing in my ears and I closed my eyes.

Please don't go alone, take me with you.

"Take me with you!" I cried.

"Mina, shhh...I'm here. Oh my god! You're drenched. Are you okay?"

River had her arms around me. She got into the covers and rubbed my arms till I felt warmth fill me again. "What happened? Why are you here?" A little dazed I tried to regain focus, as thoughts about last night invaded my mind. I couldn't believe I'd let a stranger kiss me, it was so unlike me, but he was nice. My dreams had become more vivid. Wiping away the sweat from my forehead, I placed my hand over my chest to calm myself.

"What the... River! Can you not do that?" I freaked at her, she was bouncing on the bed next to me.

"Sorry, I'm just nervous, I came to catch up, only you were sleeping. I thought I should let you wake up on your own. But then you started whimpering and crying, so I tried to wake you. What happened?" she asked, calming down.

"I don't know, it was a bad dream. I've had them a while, no biggie... Why are you here this early anyway?" I didn't want to divulge into a faceless man dream, with everything else going on right now.

"I wanted to know about you and Leo; is he right about being your mate? How was it? Did he mark you? Did you, you know? Ohmigod I'm dying here, tell me." Annoyingly, she started bouncing all over the bed again.

"Mark? What do you mean?" She settled immediately.

"You didn't do anything?" Her brown eyes widened as she questioned.

"That is none of your business!" I said, blushing as I thought of the kiss.

"Ooh, so something did happen," she stated, pinching my cheeks.

Before I could answer, Leo came in with at least ten people. He walked over with my dress from last night. "Put it on," he whispered, kissing my head. How was I to get changed? I scowled at him.

River got off the bed and used her body to shield me as I got dressed and Leo stood in front of her. I fumbled and fell over whilst dressing. Leo could've given me some warning. I felt like an idiot out of place. Standing barefooted, unwashed and with my candy floss bed hair.

"This is Mina Michaels. She is my mate. I hope to have her at my side if I decide to take the throne." As he gestured towards me, ten sets of eyes followed, whispering between themselves, which made me uncomfortable.

I've always hated any form of unwarranted attention.

A man started huffing; he seemed annoyed. He was an older man, grey haired with flecks of black, somewhat stubby and with bright rosy cheeks. "She's not your mate, I can't smell your scent on her and she definitely is not worthy of being queen. How dare you call us, *the Royal circle,* here, to her room, for this nonsense. You should have discussed it with us first," he bellowed. I didn't think such a small man could have such a loud voice; it was bouncing off my room walls. He had a point though, it would have been nice of Leo to give me some time to look presentable. And in no way was I going to be queen, he needed to get his head checked.

"Carl, I thought it best to tell you at once, and together seemed to be the obvious idea, so that we can discuss the next steps." Leo looked angry, but I couldn't figure out why. He shouldn't have been surprised by their reactions. He didn't even ask if I wanted to be Queen, he just assumed and shoved me into the deep end. What's the rush?

"There is nothing to discuss," said a brown-haired mousy woman. She was slender with a fugly, permanent frown. There wasn't even a hair out of place.

"There are standards for a queen and she does not meet them," she continued as she pointed at me with a look of pure disdain. River stepped forward, only to be pulled back forcefully by Leo.

"She? She is my mate and your future Queen! You will address her with the same respect that you address me." Leo slammed his fist into the bathroom wall and we all jumped in shock. His anger was seeping into my skin. I felt a weird pull towards him, as though we were both connected in a force field and my path only led to him. I placed my hand on his back and rested my head on his upper arm, and felt the anger slowly subside.

"I see she has an effect on you, Leo; however, she is not marked and, therefore, we have nothing to discuss. The chargé d'affaires will not be happy with this choice either. You're already aware that many of them know who she is. We see eye to eye on one thing, we do not want the late King's pet on the throne."

"If you want me, then you will do as I see fit. Mina will be the one standing next to me. That is all." Leo was seething, his tone low but clear.

"I'll leave you with a word of advice, Leo. If you have not marked her before the chargé d'affaires' minions find her, you have only put her in further danger," said the man as he walked out, closely followed by the rest of the group. I'm sure I read a threat between the lines. River followed and closed the door after them.

"You idiot! You shouldn't have put her in that position, Leo, you basically threw Mina into the snake pit without any warning!" River shouted, turning to Leo.

"I thought it was the best thing…" he tried to say before being cut off by River.

"Best thing for you, not for her. She only woke up yesterday and you're trying to push her into a world she's not ready for because YOU think it's the best thing." River had placed herself between Leo and me, and as she spoke, she poked him with every other word, which was provoking him. I could feel it. This time I didn't feel the need to calm him, more of a need to protect River, which she was having none of, as every time I tried to hold her she shook me off.

"Have you even asked Mina what she wants, or has that not occurred to you?" I felt like River and I were on the same wavelength.

"You don't get to talk to me that way, I know what's best for her." Leo's anger was starting to peak but his words were annoying me; who did he think he was? He didn't know anything about me.

"I'm right here, guys. River, calm down, I can speak for myself, and Leo, I didn't even have a recollection of you before yesterday. Just because we kissed last night doesn't mean you know me better than anyone, so get your head out of your backside." The more I spoke, the angrier I got.

"First of all, I'm going home, I need to see my parents and show them I'm still breathing." I need Clay to know I'm breathing.

"You won't be going anywhere," growled Leo.

59

"Watch me," I said, standing my ground. I could feel his weird force on my emotions. I wanted to agree with him and give in, but I would not put myself in a position where my feelings came second, ever again, so I pushed back with everything I had.

"I will send for your things, *you* don't need to go," he said, like it was final.

"I'm not just going for my things. I want to see my parents and Clay," I said, ushering River to help me pull my stuff together.

"You will not be leaving Clandestine!" Leo's voice boomed, and I was split between wanting to smack him right in the face and laughing.

"You need to remember, you don't own me. I've only just met you. Mate or not. Don't push me or I won't be coming back." I could feel my body shake with anger and I couldn't calm myself. Every cell in my body was rattling for him to make one more comment.

My words seemed to shift Leo's mood. He walked straight towards me, placed his hands on my face and apologised.

"I'm sorry, I didn't mean for it to come out the way it did. I'm just afraid that something might happen to you. I lost you a few years ago and in the process, I almost lost myself. Having you back has made me whole again, we've not had any time. If you need to go, I'll take you." He was on his knees with his arms around my waist, but his words didn't fully register. I got the apology but was distracted by the fact that something didn't feel right in me. I was still shaking, not feeling remotely comforted by his apology.

"Leo, this is difficult for me. We have to learn to adapt to each other or it won't work, whatever this is. You can't come with me; you have things of your own to deal with. River can drop me off and I will get Clay to bring me back as soon as possible. I won't be gone more than two days. Whilst I'm away, you can persuade the Royal circle and chargé d'affaires that you know what you're doing, and the Queen thing… I need to take a rain check." I knew that River would take me; we had discussed it last night before she'd left.

"Mina, I can't let you go alone. I'm sorry there's just no way." He was now getting a little irritating.

"Leo, I'm not going to tell you agai…" but before I could finish, River jumped in.

"She'll be fine. You know I can protect her and no one knows she's a therianthrope at home, so she'll be safe. Caaliyah will be coming too; in fact, she's driving." She patted Leo and grabbed my things dragging me out of the room before he could follow.

River was on the phone as we walked to the car. "I'm taking her home right now, can you let them know? Leo has put her face to face with the Royal circle without any warning and I heard an underlying threat… I don't know, he's your brother… let me drop her off and I'll come to you."

"Is that Tyler?" I asked.

"Yeah, he's furious with Leo. We both agree. He shouldn't have sprung this on you until you were ready and you accepted Leo. From a therian perspective, no one really wants an 'outsider' on the throne, which is what they'll see you as, putting you in danger."

I got into the car as Caaliyah started up the engine. We said our hellos and then she focused back on the road.

River got into the car, taking a seat beside me.

"I have to thank you for the show though, it's the first time I've seen Leo back down to anyone. He defies all authority, so I was surprised you got him to apologise. I guess you do have a weird effect on everyone, which is why the late King liked you a lot. He treated you like his own. I guess you saw things like him, the good in people.

"He also had an effect on therians pushing to overthrow him."

"I wish I remembered, River, I'm struggling to piece all this together."

"I've known you a long time, Mina, your heart and perspective of the world makes you different. You created a family between Tyler, yourself, Dermarcos and I. You never expected anything back. Even when you met Leo and things got messy, you challenged his view and made him more accepting of different people." She was holding my hand.

"Who's Demarcos?" This is the first time his name had popped up and as I said his name River squeezed my hand.

"Demarcos *was* my fiancé; he was one of the legion and Leo's friend. If you can call them that. Leo struggled to accept me as I'm a sea serpent so lower in status than a Black Panther spirit. Leo tried to persuade Demarcos into waiting for his mate, but Demarcos said he'd only ever want me in this lifetime and it was the same for me. I was rejected by my mate." River teared up but brushed them away before they could fall.

"That is the worst pain to bear, being rejected by the one created just for you. Demarcos changed that for me, he gave me hope and filled my life with love, and to top it off he gave his life to protect mine." I reached out and held her. I saw Caaliyah tear up too, but she had her eyes focused on the road and let them fall. River went through all that and survived. It spoke volumes about her strength. Losing a loved one is nothing less than heartbreaking. The rest of the drive home was in silence, and as I reached my doorstep, I said goodbye to Caaliyah and hugged River.

"Thank you for bringing me home. I'll see you soon," I said, kissing her cheek and walking in.

The familiarity of my home and the comfort it brought overwhelmed me. Walking into the living area, I saw my parents waiting with Clay. He looked like hell, worlds apart from his perfect 'boy next door' persona. He rushed towards me and scooped me up, only to be interrupted by my dad clearing his throat.

Leo's POV

She's been mumbling in her sleep and whimpering. It seems the one thing I can't protect her from is her own mind.

Her long brown locks lay across her face and shoulders as I brushed a strand away and tucked it behind her ear. Her face is a delicate oval with strong brows that frame her face and a few freckles dusted over her cute button nose.

I couldn't help but bend down and kiss her soft pink lips. She is the epitome of wonderful. Is it wrong to love like this? I'm not hurting her.

Mina. She makes my heart ache with warmth and love. Each time I see her I feel it stronger. I watch as sweat beads form on her golden skin; my palms itch to touch her but I can't.

My shirt is too big on her, yet it clings to every curve of her body. I will make her Queen! Her loyalty has always been her weakness and, therefore, she won't return to my brother.

Mina will be my Queen and I will become everything she will ever need.

Chapter Eight

"Oh… umm. Sorry," apologised Clay, as he put me down and turned red with embarrassment.

Mum stood with her arms open, allowing me to run and nestle into them. Whilst she teared up, Dad just patted my head and mumbled something along the lines of, "I'm glad you're home and safe."

My tummy rumbled, which made everyone laugh and lightened the mood. Trust my stomach to do that, but then again, I hadn't eaten anything.

After the late lunch, early dinner, we had a catch up about everything and my plans to return. My parents took it better than I expected, mostly in silence.

Clay asked whether we could go for a short drive, just to spend some time together before I returned to Clandestine, as he had something to tell me, to which I happily obliged. I missed him, not that I was going to openly admit it.

He opened the passenger side door as usual and put his hand over my head as I lowered to get in, as he's used to me always bumping my head. He seemed to know me better than I know myself, doing things before I even asked, like handing me the mp3 cable thing so that I could play my music in the car, even though he hated my musical preferences. I love to torture him with my playlist and OTT tone-deaf singing.

After a thirty-minute drive, he eventually stopped at what seemed to be the top of a hill. We were facing the entire town lights through the windscreen.

"Mina, being away from you has made me realise how much of my life you occupy. It's only been a short time and I swear it's felt like I've been walking around aimlessly. I've just been driving around looking for a special place to bring you to when you got back, to take my mind off trying to go to you. Somewhere you'll always remember and never forget."

"That's sweet, Clay, creepy but sweet." It was very thoughtful, but I don't know how to react to his open and over-the-top declaration. I looked ahead at the glistening light show in the distance but could sense him staring at me from the corner of my eye. I turned to catch him off guard and after a short period of eye contact, he turned to the back seat and picked up a cardboard box.

He reached in and pulled out a hot flask, acting as though he was a magician drawing a rabbit out of a top hat and handed it to me. I warmed my hands and smiled; I could already smell the coffee. He then handed me a heavy paper roll. Not what I was expecting, but in his defence Clay didn't usually disappoint when it came to things like this. He put the box back and took off his coat, wrapping it around my legs. For some weird reason, I started to blush.

"Are you not going to open it? I made it myself." He wanted me to open the paper roll, I was trying to mentally practice my happy face, not knowing whether I'd like the paper gift or not.

Unwrapping the top, it revealed a pancake filled with strawberries and cream. Dessert and coffee!

"Awwh Clay, you made me pancakes and coffee," I squealed.

"To be honest, I bought the pancake and just filled it with cream and strawberries. I was on a tight schedule. I'm saying that as if I would've actually made them if I had time," he laughed.

"But we can stick with what you said; I made it. Sounds better." He smirked as I lightly punched his arm. He pretended to be hurt and rubbed his bicep, making me laugh. Then again, it doesn't take much for Clay to make me laugh.

"So why this place?" I asked.

"Well, it took quite a while to find this place actually. In fact, I can't even remember how many remote places I drove to, just to find the perfect spot for you. Now give me your phone and eat your pancake," he said, winking.

I handed my phone over whilst taking a big bite out of the pancake purposefully. He played my favourite song and put the top down on his car.

"You're not cold, are you, Mina?" he asked, readjusting his coat around me.

"Just give me a hug and say you missed me already, instead of randomly touching my waist like a pervert," I said laughing.

"You wish. I already hugged you to let you know how much I missed you, and don't pretend as if you didn't feel it." He raised his brow. "And I'm only looking out for you, so you don't get cold. In fact, I'm looking out for me, cos your mum would probably kill me if you got ill."

"Why put the top down if you don't want me to be cold," I say, sticking out my tongue. Was he even thinking straight?

"Patience…" he took my coffee and pancake from me then reached over me towards my door and laid my seat flat, as if I was at the dentists. I was taken aback, pun intended; this was so unlike him.

"Lean back, Mina… All the way back. Trust me," he reassured me, with pure excitement in his eyes and a smile on his lips. I did as he said and as I faced the open sky… I was left completely mesmerised.

"Like it?" asked Clay. I barely heard what he'd said. It was a navy-blue canvas, littered with sparkling diamonds. The sky was twinkling with millions of stars. There are no words to describe how beautiful it really was. In fact, I was so lost in the moment that Clay had to repeat his question.

"Uh huh…" Looking across at Clay, I saw his green eyes focused on me.

"How did you even find this place?" I asked, completely in awe.

"I know you like stars and I like stars… so I just took that and then set out to find some mutual ground, literally, where we could relish our favourite pastime. I couldn't speak to you or see you whilst you were away and all I knew was that you were injured. Mina, it was driving me crazy 'cause I didn't know what had happened or if you were okay. You're my bestest friend. If anything happened to you, I don't know what I would have done." He was babbling on, which was new; Clay doesn't babble.

"Clay, I'm okay and thank you for caring. Thank you, I really needed it," I said, putting my hand on the back of his. He turned his hand round and locked his fingers around mine. Looking up at him it hit me, why didn't I see it before? I could see for the first time how he felt, and all at once, every moment spent with Clay flashed back with a different perspective.

"Clay…I'm…erm," he interrupted me before I could say anything.

"I know…" He knows what?

"I'm not expecting anything, Mina, I swear! I don't know what happened or how it happened. I realised after I got Tyler's call. He told me you'd got hurt and in that moment my heart hurt like it never had before. I just wanted you to know that I love you. I really do. I somehow always have, and I think I always will. Nothing will change that."

The sincerity in his voice made me cry out. The tears started to flow. Why didn't he say anything? "How do you know Tyler?" was the only question that seemed relevant in the moment that my best friend confessed his love to me. Had I no words in return?

"Tyler and I have been friends since we were kids. We're closer than most people think. He's like a brother," he said reassuringly, giving my hand a squeeze and wiping away my tears.

"Mina, I want to ask you something. Don't jump in with your answer. Take some time to think about it. I've made my decision. For the last five years I've found a happiness that I didn't think I ever could." Oh no…

"Please don't ask me to marry you… too much, too fast!" He just burst out in howls of laughter and I felt my cheeks turn red.

"Who knew you had a vivid imagination. I just wanted to ask whether I could come back with you? I don't think I can be away from you. The last few weeks have almost killed me. Tyler said it would be fine and you could do with a familiar face." Did Clay just ask to move with me? He'd definitely eaten something funny.

"I err…wait…what do you even mean? Your whole life is here?" I wanted him to, obviously. With Clay around, it would feel like home and I trusted him, with everything that has been going on… I needed him, and now he was telling me he wanted to move with me.

"Yes, in a way, but I think my life is only here because you were here. When you first got hurt, Tyler brought you to me because he trusted me, more so than Leo or anyone else. Seeing you pick yourself up and start again made me want to protect you. You were like a child learning everything and then the way you depended on me and smiled every time you saw me… I didn't see that before." His eyes were overflowing with unconditional love.

"Yes!" I shouted.

"Yes?" His eyes lit up questioningly.

"Yes, I accept. I need you in my life. Over the last few days, all I've been thinking about is how you would make me understand all this and how I wouldn't be alone. Selfish on my part, I know, but…" Before I could finish my sentence, he leaned in and hugged me. Arms hanging straight, I wasn't expecting it…but it was the warmest hug I'd had in a long time and I couldn't help but hug right back. After letting go, he snuck a kiss on my cheek, to which I exclaimed: "CLAY!"

"What? I just really, really missed you!" he retorted.

"Uh huh." What is it with boys kissing me suddenly, like hello Clay, where were you before Jesse?

"I love you, Mina."

"I love me too."

We lay back and watched the sky in silence for a long while.

I slept through the night like a baby, which hadn't happened in a couple of months. I guess I felt a lot more settled now that I knew Clay would be with me.

Now I just needed to tell him I'm a Therianthrope.

Clay's POV

I couldn't stop myself from pacing the room. The Michaels were sitting patiently waiting for Mina to come home. I just needed to see her, hold her and never let her out of my sight.

Derek Michaels walked over and placed his hand on my shoulder, moving me to a seat next to him. As I sat down, my leg started to shake. When would she get here?

The door started to move, and I held my breath, thinking she's here.

As she walked in through the door, my heart leapt. There's my girl!

Chapter Nine

Last night, after I got home, I looked back on all my memories over the last five years and I couldn't believe the situation. Clay had always been by my side, from the moment I woke up. How did I not notice that every issue, every breakdown, nightmare, panic attack or bump in the road was solved by him?

These thoughts stayed with me whilst I walked around my room, picking things up and throwing them in to my cases. He was on his way already, so I needed to finish packing.

Mum and Dad came in a few minutes ago, just to check up on me and give me 'parental' advice on being safe and coming straight back if I ever needed to. They aren't overly emotional, which I love. They're there to support me but don't smother.

"Knock knock." Clay's voice filled my bedroom.

"You do know you don't have to say knock knock whilst knocking?" I said.

"You do know I don't need your permission to do anything," he replied.

What could I say to that? I stuck out my tongue, which made him chuckle.

He started to help me pack. I saw an eye roll here and there as I kept putting things in and taking them out again, but he didn't say anything. Before I uprooted him, I needed to tell him that I'm not human. Well, I am human, but more than human. What? I can't even explain it to myself, how am I going to explain it to him?

Sitting on my suitcase whilst Clay zipped it up, I just went for it.

"Clay, I'm a human not human spirit animal thing type, a therianthrope." Exhaling after I'd finished, he just continued zipping up and looked at me. Perched on top of my suitcase, his arms were at either side, with me in the middle. He just stared at me for a while, watching, his green eyes focused on me. It weirded me out a little. His gaze was way too intense. I think his declaration last night had got to his head a little and now I was blushing.

Great!

"Stop it," I said, trying to bat away his gaze. He was enjoying it, the turd.

"Do I make you nervous, Mina?" he smiled smugly.

"Only in your head, you dimwit! You're just being creepy; did you even hear what I said?" I knocked his head a little; ego is not a good look on my best friend.

"I know what you are. Tyler's my friend, remember? I know what he is too. I've known from the moment I met you, so don't worry. I know what I'm getting into." He helped me up and headed for the door with my stuff. "Erm, okay…" What else can I say? He knew.

Looking around my room one last time, I grabbed my shoes and handbag and followed Clay as he lugged my cases down the stairs. He filled the boot of his car and talked on the phone whilst I hugged my parents and said goodbye.

"I'll be fine, don't worry. Clay is going to be with me. I love you both so much, more than you'll know."

The drive was peaceful. I felt content, Clay had literally filled his car with junk food to keep me quiet and I was happy; it was like going on an adventure with my best friend.

"Are you sure about leaving everything and entering a world of crazy? Trust me, it's all so bizarre that sometimes I doubt I'm actually awake." I need him to be sure; it's not exactly going to be a walk in the park. Clay can take care of himself but when it comes to therian shape shifters with speed and strength on their side, I don't see him boding well.

"Mina, it's simple for me. Do you want me there?" he sent me a quick glance before focusing back on the road.

"Uh huh!" As much as I want to say no, I can't lie. I want Clay with me.

"Then I'm coming and staying," he winked.

"How are we going to explain a non-spirit? From what I know, it's all cloak and dagger and there are a lot of rules about keeping the therian world concealed from all non-spirits.

"Don't worry; Tyler and I have that covered. As long as we stay out of trouble and I don't attract too much attention, we're all good." It's odd that my best friend is friends with my childhood best friend. How small is the world?

We were about a third of the way into the drive when Clay started to act weird.

"We may have to take a detour bestie," he said, looking at the rearview mirror. He then turned to look over his shoulder.

He dialled a number which was saved under 'Alpha'.

"Where are you? Is Mina with you?" The voice sent tingles down my spine, it's the guy.

"Tyler, we're on the way but I've been tailed since we left the house. I didn't notice till a few minutes ago, are they coming for her?" Clay reached out and squeezed my hand.

"Get her to safety… I'm coming. Go somewhere she can be concealed, like dense trees or something. Clay, keep her safe till I get there, you know what to do." With that, Tyler was gone.

"That was Tyler?" I asked, still unable to shake the tingles.

"Are you okay? You tensed when you heard his voice. Do you recognise it?"

"No, it was just that you said they're coming for me, who's they?" I'm lying to my best friend. But then again, it's not like I can explain what I just felt in actual words. He was speeding up, keeping his eyes on the cars behind us.

"I won't let anything happen to you. I know a place a little further out. I used to camp out there, a conserved woodland area.

"Great, woodlands, as nothing creepy ever happens in them!" Why can't I catch a break?

"I'm trying here, I also know Tyler… He won't let anything happen to you and neither will I." I don't know how, but the two cars that were behind us had moved either side of our car. They had tinted windows, so I couldn't get a look in. I should be freaking out as usual, but I just felt a rush of adrenaline pumping through my veins. We were doing over ninety miles an hour. Luckily, the roads were practically empty. I don't know where Clay was taking us as he suddenly went off road. The cars started colliding into us, which riled me more than anything; I know I should be frightened, but it was simply getting on my nerves.

"Things will start to get a bit bumpy. Tyler let me know about the danger you have been put in, with Leo thinking you'll

71

take the throne, without even asking you. He's an idiot—acts first, thinks later. Really gets under my skin. I just didn't think how fast that danger might come." As he said that, the car on the left smashed into us, spinning us around and making me scream. Clay regained control quickly, his reflexes were amazing.

"Move away from them before we get killed," I shouted.

"Shouting doesn't help, Mina, can't you see I'm trying?" he said, whilst steering away from them and racing ahead, he put some distance between us and them.

About half a mile later we stopped at an opening of woodland. Clay got out of the car and dragged me out of my seat.

"You need to run into the forest as fast as you can," he said, shoving me towards the woods.

"I'm not leaving you, Clay," I replied as the cars got closer.

"I have no time to argue with you. You need to run, no matter what, keep running. I can keep myself safe, it's you they want." I was not leaving him, I didn't even know who they were.

"I can't…"

"I am NOT going to tell you again. Run!" I had never seen Clay this mad. Didn't he understand that he could die?

I started to run; I, the klutz with two left feet who gave up running probably after the age of twelve. It was more of a jog than a run, and that's when I heard the earth-shattering scream that stopped me in my tracks.

It belonged to Clay. I wanted to turn back and have a look .but there was a voice in my head that kept telling me to run, so I did. I ran head first into someone, which made me shriek and flail about like a fish out of water. His hand reached out and covered my mouth, making me freak out.

"Calm down…breathe… I'm not going to hurt you." As his voice registered, I began to inhale his scent and let it envelop me—a scent I knew and craved.

"I err… You're…err…him…" Was I stammering because of Tyler or because I needed to catch my breath? Or both?

"Tyler! My name is Tyler."

Clay's POV

I've struggled the past few weeks without Mina. When she was with Jesse, it bugged me. I hated seeing them together, but I've only just realised why. She keeps me grounded, while other

72

girls throw themselves at me. Mina, she never looked at me like that, not once. At first, I was annoyed, it bugged me that she didn't find me attractive, it even bruised my ego somewhat. I have my pride.

Then, I saw how she was with me, compared to everyone else. Whenever we went out, she didn't drift. She was in my close vicinity and always looked around to see where I was and smiled with relief when her eyes landed on me.

Slowly, without noticing, I did the same. I watched out to see if she was looking for me and found myself gravitating toward her. It became a habit. Then she met Jesse and things changed. He was always around her and whenever she looked for me, or me for her, he blocked her view. Knowingly.

We banged heads a few times over my friendship with her, but he disgusted me. Jesse knew she struggled to let people get close, she hated being touched and he used that against her. He told all the lads that she gave him free reign because of her issues. I knew it wasn't true. I also knew she didn't know he told everyone, and as soon as he said it, he regretted it, but it was too late.

That's one of the reasons I can't let her go alone; Tyler won't always be around and boys will take advantage of her naivety and kindness and she doesn't get it. She's hopeless in that department. More than that, she is okay about close contact with me… like it's normal. She doesn't recoil in disgust when I cuddle her, but she doesn't realise it. Maybe she feels something? If she doesn't, I'll wait till she does. I've had my fun. My focus now is Mina and her happiness.

Chapter Ten

My voice stuck in my throat. As I looked at him, I couldn't even remember my own name to introduce myself. His hazel grey-coloured eyes bore into mine. They were lined with some guy liner and had both a glint of danger and sparkle that held my gaze. His hair surprised me the most…it was thick, silvery charcoal and long. It's not really a look I would've put on a guy, but he looks good. Great, in fact. His nose was straight, and he had soft, full lips. Pink and plump. These brothers have won the lottery in the gene pool, but they look nothing alike. Tyler is beautiful!

"Don't look at me like that." he said, taking a step back, snapping me back to reality.

"I need to go get Clay!" I murmured, turning back the way I'd come.

"Clay can find his own way to us. We need to keep moving. Those people, they're here for you, not him." I could see a similarity between the brothers. They had a knack for talking down at people and telling them what to do.

"You don't need to tell me what to do," I retorted.

"Well, you can stay out here till they find you then. I don't exactly care." Yeah right, he doesn't care. Does he think I don't know who he is? I recognised his voice and scent from the two previous times.

"Oh, Tyler! Please don't leave me on my own, I need you!" .I exclaimed with as much emphasis as possible.

"Great, sarcasm! It's just what I need right now. I ran straight here for your ungrateful behind. So don't push me," he said. Why was he annoyed?

"Oh, my princess in tinfoil," I said, putting my hands together and fluttering my eyelashes, trying to sound like a damsel in distress—'trying' being the operative word. "Thank

74

you for coming all this way even though I didn't ask you to," I stated, rolling my eyes.

"Princess? In tinfoil?" he repeated, raising his brows. He slowly started to walk towards me, not moving his gaze from mine, before suddenly shoving me up against a tree and pressing himself against me, holding me in place. I started to squirm, and he just knocked my back against the trunk.

"Shut up and stop moving. They're here," he hissed. All I could hear was the thundering beat of his heart as his chest was pressed against my face. There were rustling sounds close by, not that I could focus on them. The forest was dense, so I didn't have a clear view of where the sound was coming from and there was covering from other trees. Tyler's body blocked most of my view anyway. We stood in silence for so long that my legs started to wobble. He must have felt my legs give way as his hands found their way to my waist to hold me up. I had no choice but to lean into his hands for support; the tingly sensation coursing through my body was making me breathe faster. Tyler took a few steps back.

"Did you even wash your hair? It smells like cheese," he commented, turning away from me and clenching his fists. Was this guy for real?

"I washed my hair! And for your information, we were in a car chase whilst I was eating cheese puffs, you jerk!" I exclaimed through gritted teeth.

"I told you that your foodie habit will gain you some pounds. I wasn't wrong," he said looking down at me.

"Get the hell away from me, you creep, no one's commenting on how feminine your face is for your body!" I was angry, why? I have always been self-conscious, but not unhappy with the way I look or my size. Yes, I'm a little curvier than most girls my height, but I love how I feel in my own skin.

"I didn't mean to offend you. It's just an observation," he´ said, laughing.

"Observe this," I said, sticking up my finger whilst walking away. The guy was an imbecile, and I thought there was something between us, but his personality sucks.

"Mina, we can't leave until Clay is here. Our priority is getting you back to Clandestine safe and I can't do that whilst you're stomping around attracting attention." He followed me while I tried to put distance between us. "I'm not stomping, I'm walking. I can't help the fact that I've *gained the pounds,* as you so eloquently put it. Whilst we wait for Clay please don't talk to me, and stay far away from me." I sat down on a thick root of a nearby tree. It was uncomfortable but hey, I was in a fricking forest! Not gonna find anywhere better. I didn't need to give Tyler any more reason to make comments by clumsily falling over myself, so I was just going to…sit.

"So, a few years away from us; was life good?" he probed.

"I said no talking," I replied, which made him sigh.

"Believe it or not, we used to be close, Mina. You and I, closer than anyone else. Before my brother, before things became all about power and having to choose between us and the right thing. We were both different back then. You were more inclined to take my side all the time." Was he seriously trying to build up an understanding after making me feel like a fat hippo, stomping around? Or tell me we were an 'us' once?

"I very much doubt it. And even if we were, I guess life changed us…"

"We used to get under each other's skin, which I see still comes naturally to us," he chuckled. As he laughed I was distracted by his dimple. When he was silent he was handsome in a pretty way. In fact, annoyingly dreamy, and now I wasn't even mad at him for calling me a fatso.

"I can't imagine taking your side. When you speak to me, I just want to smack you, preferably with a large frying pan," I stated.

"I didn't call you fat!" he said.

"What?" I didn't even say that.

The hair on the back of my neck started to prickle, making me immediately stand. Tyler ran in front of me as we were surrounded by guys in hooded robes, carrying some old looking swords. They looked like they walked out of an old martial arts movie.

"Tyler, we have no argument with you. Just give us the girl." Why are they holding old swords?

"Sorry, boys. I can't let you have what's mine. I don't share!" Tyler's tone was playful, but there was an edge to it that sent tingles up my spine.

"If you know what's good for you, you'll walk away. I don't want to have to hurt you."

As Tyler spoke, he started to undress. First his jacket, then shirt; thankfully, he left his pants on and his wrists were covered by large metallic cuffs like you'd find on 'a gladiator in Rome'. Didn't realise that was a look; everything about him was put together weirdly, but it didn't look out of place. His back was wide and strong, and I could see scars trailing down it. The sun was seeping through the trees, highlighting the unevenness on his back, but as he turned there was an image of the back of a girl with windswept hair etched on his left peck. She was sitting on a huge dog... No, a wolf, with Luna written under it. His body was muscular. Larger than Leo's and so much more defined. Why was I comparing? It wasn't even a competition.

One of the men turned to me and said something completely foreign which resulted in Tyler swinging for him. Everything became a little hazy then, the movements were too fast and rushed. It was three against one. They charged at him all at once, their swords blocked by his cuffs. I could see why he's wearing them now.

Tyler blocked every strike to begin with. They kept coming at him, always together, so it wasn't really a fair fight. One was aimed at me, but Tyler got in the way, blocking it with his body, earning him an open slit on his back. His eyes locked onto mine and he didn't even blink when the sword made contact. But his reflexes slowed, and he wasn't as quick to block them, earning him a few gashes on his arms. He somehow disarmed his assailants of their weapons, but it wasn't enough to beat them.

Tyler could hold his own. He was doing some acrobatic stuff, but he got slower with every blow he received, and I could see him getting weaker. I wanted to help in some way, but I was glued to the spot behind him. Tyler spat out blood every few minutes like it was nothing, and by the end, the three men were more injured than he was and left cowering on the floor. Tyler picked up his things and walked towards me, when I saw a few more men turn up behind him. There's no way we'd make it out of this forest.

"Tyler, behind you," I whispered.

He looked at me with a bloodied mouth and a cut above his eye. This guy was going to die if I didn't do something.

"Wait. Stop! All of you stop, please!" I screamed, halting them from moving any closer to him.

"I'll go with you, if you let Tyler leave first." There's no way I'll let him die because of me; it's my turn to save him.

"Shut up! I'm not leaving. If they want you, they'll have to go through me," he said, coming close enough that I could see his body already changing colour in the places where he'd been hit.

"Stop trying to play the hero and leave. I don't need you to fight my battles; we barely even know each other." I knew that if he didn't back away from me, I was going to have to kick him in the groin and then run and hope the guys followed.

"You're playing with my patience, Mina. Don't move and just wait, trust me." He then smiled, an actual smile during the fight; a smile that held me in my place. Tyler looked around like he was focusing hard. He may have been hit on the head as he was squinting.

From the moment that we met, I felt an urge to be around him, even without knowing who he was, and now his smile had connected me to him further. That smile was just for me. I felt something I had never felt before. My feelings for him, what were they? Images of Jesse flashed into my mind and I felt sick with guilt, like I had cheated on Tyler.

"Just remember, I offered you the opportunity to leave," said Tyler, before letting out a howl. It was a deafening sound, but it was beautiful and sent chills up *my* spine. The sound echoed throughout the forest, and in the silence which followed, similar howls struck up in reply. I got a sense of déjà vu.

The forest started to move on either side and I could feel the ground beneath me tremble. The men, who were now nine in total, looked around and backed themselves into a circle with their backs to one another. Out of nowhere, I saw a guy leap through the air. He landed in a bundle right in front of us.

"Clay! Are you okay, what happened?" He was followed by some big wolves and wolfmen. By some, I mean like a hundred.

"I'm okay. Just needed to get some reinforcements. Sorry, I'm late to the party," he said looking back. He had a gnarly bite on his shoulder. Blood was seeping through his top all the way down to his sleeve and the chunky jagged flesh was enough to bring up the contents of my stomach. I couldn't hold back and turned around to puke on the spot.

"Mina!" yelled Clay with concern. The guy has blood draining from him and a little puke seems like the end of the world.

"I'm OK," I reassured him. Tyler stepped forward as Clay walked towards me. They shook forearms and Clay whispered something to him.

"Stand down before my pack tear you to shreds," Tyler's voice echoed around the forest, followed by growls from the wolves.

"You don't need to watch this, Mina." Clay's voice brought my focus back to him. I could smell the metallic scent that was coming from him, making me hold my nose.

"Are you okay?" I asked looking at him. He smiled and nodded.

"That's just a scratch. I'm fine. Are you okay? You're not hurt, are you?" he asked, ruffling my hair. A scratch? He said it's a scratch when I could see down to his bone.

"I'm fine. What happened to you?" Who had bitten him and why was he thrown at us?

He laughed, "I knew that wherever Tyler is, his pack goes. I needed to create enough distraction for them to get here on time. The guys back at the car were wolf rogues, they didn't take kindly to being played, and to get to you I needed a boost. So I asked the betas to help me out." He shrugged like it was nothing.

The wolves growled louder. Clay and I turned towards them to see one of the nine had silently made his way to us and had his blade pointed towards me, which had set Tyler and his pack into a frenzy. The guy was saying something in another language and Tyler was responding. They were both angry and agitated.

Tyler rushed to grab the guy by his neck and lifted him off the ground, and as he did, the guy pushed his sword down into Tyler's right shoulder, all the way down. Tyler didn't even flinch. The howls from his pack sounded as if they were in pain. It hurt to hear them. He threw the guy down hard, and I heard a few bones crack. He spoke to the rest of them as a couple helped him up and he rejoined the circle.

As they all turned towards me, one spoke.

"You may think you're safe, but this is just the beginning. If Leo wants to put you on the throne, it will be your dead body. The Royal family were slaughtered because we needed a stronger rule, one where the understanding of pure bloodlines is the most fundamental aspect. They will come for you and will keep coming till our mission is complete and a new era is born, where pure breeds are the only ones left and non-spirits bow down to us." He then shouted in a foreign tongue and all nine men slit each other's throats and fell lifeless. A piercing scream invaded my ears, filling me with dread, and I broke out in a cold sweat. I was shaking from fear.

My vision blurred and when I closed my eyes, I felt two firm hands on either side of my face.

"Mina, look at me, it's okay. Look at me." Opening my eyes, I could see concern-filled green eyes. As soon as I focused, I realised the scream was coming from me. Immediately shutting my mouth, I cut the sound off. Clay had me in his arms. He picked me up and started walking through the forest, and in the background, I heard Tyler shout some sort of orders.

Tyler's POV

The way she looks at me drives me crazy, doesn't she know I am fighting all my instincts, when she looks at me like that I know there's no one else in her view. Leo removed her memories selfishly. It was not only for her own safety; he wanted me to be erased. So, I can't just expect Mina to know what we had, what we have. She's mine, always has been.

It's foolish but I want her to have our memories, to know how close we were, how I felt about her. She felt the same about me too. I knew it!

Leo entered her life and I became a coward, hiding my feelings, trying to push her away, thinking he could protect her. In time, I became jealous of how she looked at him and gave up. I couldn't bear the thought of her with anyone, never mind my brother.

Right now, she's back in my life, here before my eyes. Her beauty shatters me to my core. The large doe-like eyes always glisten and stare into my soul like no other woman has, her cute button nose scrunches up when she tries to concentrate and those lips—the way they smile stops me in my tracks.

She's always been a little on the curvy side, her skirt and jumper clinging in the right places like a second skin. Man, the things she makes me feel drive me insane. I hated how the clothes fit her. Having her in my arms for just a moment made me lose control of my senses. If she asked for the moon, I'd be stupid enough to attempt to pluck it from the sky just for her.

My wolf is crazy for his Luna, so much so that if I let him take the reins, no man would stand between us, not even my brother.

Chapter Eleven

I was being carried, and slightly opening one eye, I looked up and saw Tyler's face instead of Clay's. This made me jerk up in his arms. I completely misjudged the situation as my head hit Tyler's jaw. He dropped me to the ground.

"What the hell, Mina!" I didn't mean to hit his jaw, I was trying to get off him.

"I'm sorry; you shocked me. You and Clay shouldn't have played pass the parcel with me," I tried to explain. "He had things to do and didn't want to wake you up. Trust me, I didn't want to carry you either. You weigh a ton," he said.

"You're such a dog," I said scowling.

"I'm actually a wolf but let's go with dog for now," he smirked.

"Arrrrgggh!" He made me think of multiple eff word combinations I so wanted to use. *Breathe...you're a lady*, I thought. *Don't let him affect you.*

Purposefully stomping away, I walked into multiple brawny guys to the amusement of Tyler who just clapped.

"Luna? Are you okay?" The guys tried to check me over, as though I was a child.

"Erm, my name is Mina, not Luna."

"My name is Angelico De Mattea. I'm one of Tyler's Betas, you are our Luna." I don't get it, but all the rest of the guys surrounding me lowered their heads. They were all huge and not once did I feel threatened, more like protected. It's a feeling I could get used to. I don't know why, but I reached out and put my hand through Angelico's hair. I wasn't trying to be condescending, but for some reason I needed to do that, and he moved into it, like I was more than an equal.

"That's because you're not their equal, you're their leader," Tyler whispered. He followed this with a growl that made the guys scatter and I immediately removed my hand.

"Jeez, give a girl some warning; you scared me." It was his proximity that scared me. He was being familiar, and it was throwing me off. I didn't need any further boy complications after what Clay had said.

"And what did he say?" Tyler asked, eyeing me up.

He's answering my thoughts? Wait...what? Tyler just smirked.

Can you hear me? I said in my head, feeling more than a little stupid. He nodded, which threw me for six. *How?*

"You're part of my pack. I can hear all your thoughts, since we've been young. You let me in. Every time you fell into a ditch or got lost, you called for me," he said, walking us towards a camp fire.

The pack were in groups, eating and chattering away. I saw their eyes follow us and whenever I looked at one of them they beamed a smile that warmed my entire being. I felt love and respect seep into my skin.

"Look at them, this is your pack. Your family, they chose you and you them." Watching the animated actions and hearing the laughter from these men gave me a sense of belonging.

"Why did they choose me?" I was really curious as to why a group of wolves would want a girl with two left feet and no hand-eye coordination to lead them. I mean they're equipped to look after themselves.

"Your heart, your resilience and your loyalty to them. These men were animals at best, we're built to be hunters, emotionless and your nurturing ways changed them. You brought out their goodness and became the light in their darkness, in all our darkness. Being a wolf is lonely without a mate. These men chose to wait till this mission, or whatever else you want to call it, is complete. They owe you their lives, we all do." How? It made no sense to me.

"You lost a part of yourself years ago, but we'll work with you to get it back. Trust us," Tyler continued.

"I thought wolf packs are usually small?" I asked.

"We combined packs, most of the Alpha's were killed during the siege of the Royal family. We were part of the legion. Lives 'were lost, and you connected us all; you were willing to sacrifice it all for us."

"Are they all from Clandestine?" I was interested in filling in my blanks and figuring out who these men chose to be loyal to.

"We all went through Clandestine as recruits, but we are all active now. We have our own places and positions around the world. I still use Clandestine as my base because of my cover. It's easier to be part of a known arts company, even if it is a front." *I didn't peg you as the artsy type*, I giggled in my mind.

"We're getting along, don't make me remind you of how distracting your face is." My face? He's playing a game to make me blush.

"I meant your makeup-less face. We can work on your appearance when we get back to Clandestine." Giving him the best death stare I could, I went around the pack, walking through the different groups as they greeted me with warmth. By the end of it, I had become fond of the word Luna. I wanted to protect these men, even though I knew I couldn't. They could protect themselves better than I ever could.

"You're wrong, Mina. You make them stronger." Tyler was right behind me again. Does this guy not understand what personal space is?

"Not when your life is on the line!" he whispered and disappeared, leaving me feeling dreary. I half expected a witty retort. I kept talking about wanting a simple life, but my life wasn't simple to begin with and I don't think I'd want to go back now, knowing what I do, irrespective of how out of this world it is. I'd like to keep Leo, River, Clay, Tyler and the pack in my life.

"You're being hard on him, bestie." Clay decided to make an appearance.

"Where have you been? Where did you go?" I hadn't seen him since he'd carried me earlier.

"I had to run some errands. Leo is having a mental breakdown as he didn't want you out of his sight."

It's so weird to have my best friend here, helping me out in the weirdest situations and he's not even phased by it all.

"Leo needs to realise my life is my own. I make the decisions. Even if he is my mate," I huffed.

"He's not your mate," he mumbled.

"I get the feeling you don't like him," I said.

"What's there to like?" he replied.

"I don't know, he cares about me, maybe even has feelings for me." Clay just made retching sounds.

"You only feel something because his animal spirit is strong, and he literally forces it on yours." Even though I've seen a sea serpent and a hundred plus wolves, I didn't think I'd ever get used to this kind of conversation.

"What does that mean?" Forcing his spirit animal?

"You're a therianthrope, quite possibly a powerful one. Your spirit needs an equally powerful mate. Leo's a lion, the strongest of his kind, but he uses it to his advantage. He wants you as his mate. I accept he loves you, but it's also about his ego and pride. Tyler's a hybrid, the Alpha of the biggest pack in the world. His lycan spirit is fierce and powerful, but he's never made his animal spirit call yours. He wants it to be your choice while you are in your human form—your weakest and most vulnerable form—to make the choice with a clear mind, without your spirit animal getting involved. He wants your love, not just the mating process." I have a lot to learn about the Kang brothers.

"Is that why I find it difficult to think around Leo?" Is he forcing me to like him? Is that why I threw up after he kissed me?

"Yes, he lets his animal form come to the surface around you, which messes with your senses. He just doesn't want to lose out to Tyler and isn't willing to play fair, he's not forcing you to like him as for the spirit bonding to work there has to be some feelings involved, he's just making you think yours are stronger than they actually are. You were Tyler's first love. You let him follow you around like a lost puppy growing up. Everyone talks about the young love you shared and then Leo came into the picture and wanted you for himself, so he started using his spirit to attract you. At the time, Leo's spirit was complete with him and he could control it. He used that to his advantage because Tyler was still training to control his wolf.

"So that's why you think Leo's your mate, but you haven't given Tyler a fair chance and he won't ever push you. He thought it was best to walk away because you were happy and that's all he wanted."

My heart dropped.

"Clay, what do I do?" I could feel the difference that existed in the pull towards Tyler and Leo.

"You're asking me? I can't advise you. Not when I feel how I do about you, I just want you to be happy." He wrapped me up in a hug, and as I reached up, I recalled his shoulder bite and stopped, not wanting to hurt him.

"How are you? Is your shoulder hurting?" I asked trying to not look for his bite mark.

"I'm as fit as a fiddle. Tyler healed me with his blood." He did what?

"What do you mean, he healed you with his blood?" I pushed.

"I told you, Tyler is strong. His wolf is on another level, his blood can heal his pack, but it drains his energy. His wound hasn't even healed yet and he gave me his blood even though it's made him worse." I could see the respect and admiration Clay had for Tyler.

"Where is Tyler?" I asked, and Clay just pointed towards the trees.

"Hurry up, we need to head to Clandestine before Leo sends out a search party and I don't want you standing between the two brothers." I really didn't need a search party.

Entering the opening, I could see Tyler sitting on a tree stump, wincing as he tried to wrap some sort of bandage around himself. He stopped as soon as he heard me and turned to look.

"Who doesn't understand personal space now?" he questioned.

"I didn't realise a grown man would get touchy over a comment like that," I said walking over and sitting next to him.

The cut in his shoulder was clean and had completely gone through and then out again the other side.

"You healed Clay, yet you didn't heal yourself, isn't that a little silly?" I asked.

"I'm alpha, I don't want to use the pack's power to heal myself and weaken them," he said looking at me. He was more thoughtful than he looked. He could carry the responsibility of more than a hundred men and look out for them, yet he couldn't be nice to me.

"Teasing you is my hobby," he smiled.

"Can you get out of my head?" I scowled.

"Okay, but you're so loud it's distracting at times." I couldn't help myself. I punched him and then regretted it immediately afterwards as his wound opened making him wince.

"You should have avoided the blade, you're so cocky that you don't seem to care about your own safety at times," I say out loud.

"I couldn't avoid it; don't you think I would have if I could? I was angry that he wasn't giving me the information I needed." I could hear the frustration creeping up into his voice.

"The information was about me, right?" He just looked at me, answering my question with his silence.

"Tyler, you don't have to endanger yourself for me. It's not worth it." He grunted.

"You don't know what you're worth, so you have no room to speak. The more you try to avoid help and do things yourself, the more you put us in difficulty." He could have a point; I didn't know enough, not yet, and maybe I needed to listen until I figured this out.

"That's a first, you listening, I mean," he said. I'm sure I told him to not invade my thoughts. Why does this guy always do the opposite? He was infuriating.

"If you keep feeling like that, you'll soon fall for me!" he grinned, earning himself a smack around the head.

"You're annoying," I stated.

"I know, but only to you," he replied, smiling, before saying I was distracting him. I offered to help clean and wrap his cuts.

The open wound on his shoulder was now dripping blood down his back. In the moonlight, I could see all of his other cuts and scars clearly. Some looked like ragged blade marks and the others were bites.

How can he be okay with all those scars? When did he receive his first one? How much pain has he endured? Subconsciously, my hand was tracing his scars. I only realised this when I felt Tyler's back tense beneath my fingertips. His silence was a first too. I guess there's a way to keep him quiet. My hand found its way to one of his newest editions.

Tyler's attitude towards me was partly my fault; I hurt him without knowing. If only I could remove that heartbreak. My lips found their way to his wound and as the metallic taste of blood

87

entered my mouth, Tyler let out a rough growl and stood up, almost knocking me off the stump. His eyes were dark as he grabbed my arm and lifted me up. I felt his nails dig into my wrist and for a minute I saw us, in my mind. Happy.

Tyler's POV

The promise I've been keeping is becoming too much for me. Ever since Mina came back to Clandestine it's been playing on my mind. It's her secret, her truth. She needs to know before it's too late, but can I break my word to the king?

What do I do? I want to come clean and tell Mina everything, but what if she can't handle it? I don't want to push her away or give her such a big responsibility that she will struggle to carry the burden.

On the other hand, if I don't tell her, she might not find her true self. She may follow Leo blindly because she doesn't realise who she is. The last Royal, my Luna, my Queen.

Chapter Twelve

"Don't be afraid of what's to come, Mina; regardless of what you choose, I will always be here if you need me." Tyler had his arms wrapped around me from behind, but for some reason the moment was filled with unexplainable sadness.

"They say it has to be Leo. I have to stay by his side, it's what my father would want, but I don't know how I feel." My father always told me to follow my heart. So, am I doing the right thing?

"You'll know if it's right in time. Just take it slow and stay close to Leo. Don't ever allow yourself to get hurt." He was going to leave.

"You're leaving me, aren't you?" I asked holding his arms tighter.

"I can't see you every day and not want to be with you. Leo won't appreciate it and we can't afford to let our guard down. You need to be protected till you change. I'll come back for you when I know I can protect you, and if you still want me, I'll fight to be with you." With that, he let go.

Snapping back to reality, it dawned on me that Tyler and I had much more than what people think. I wanted to know what happened, why I picked Leo when I clearly had feelings for Tyler. He released my wrist, which now had small cuts where his claws had sunk in.

"I'm so sorry, Mina, I don't know what happened. When you kissed my cut, I just reacted. I'm sorry." It was my fault.

"Don't worry, it didn't hurt. Tyler, your wounds." As I tried to figure out how he healed, Tyler reached out to touch his shoulder where the blade entered. There wasn't even the faintest scar, he'd healed completely as though nothing had happened.

"It must be you! You healed me, but how?" He looked shocked.

"Wait, how can it be me? I don't understand." Does it mean…am I a wolf too?

"No, you're not a wolf. I'm not sure how much everyone's told you, but you have more than one animal spirit. You can encompass them all, but you get to choose your power spirit. Your bloodline is one of a kind, not many people know that about you. Mina, you can pick and choose the animal traits you want. If the people who are after you find out before you shift, the target on your back will be bigger and worth a lot more. You can't tell anyone!" Woah, info overload. How does he know all this about me?

"I will tell you next time; too much has happened today."

"Do you think I'm meant to be with Leo?" I don't know why I blurted that out.

"It's not about what I or anyone else thinks; it's about you and who you choose," he said.

"Why haven't you let your wolf connect with whatever my spirit is?"

"I don't want to confuse you even if…" He smiled, trailing off and flashing his dimple, which was so distracting. The speckle of hair on his jaw was even more so. Tyler's laughter invaded my ears.

"You said you wouldn't listen to my thoughts," I said, standing up and facing him, praying there wasn't any colour in my cheeks.

"You're literally screaming it in your head. I didn't realise how bad you want me." He winked at me, making me grumble.

"I don't want you, I just know how to appreciate pretty. You're pretty." I'd lost it.

"Sure, I can clearly see you don't want me." He walked over to me, making me panic a little, but I didn't want to let him win by backing down.

"It's not me who wants you. It's you who wants me. I saw the way you looked at me before," I replied, trying to stand my ground.

"Don't flatter yourself, Mina. In my position, any guy would've done the same. No one asked you to kiss my back."

"I…err." I didn't mean to kiss his back; I don't know what happened. He was hurt because of me. I could feel my eyes stinging. I needed to go and find Clay, get back to Clandestine and not cause myself further embarrassment.

Before I took two steps, I felt Tyler's arms around me, giving me flashbacks of walking around a rose garden. "I'm sorry. I didn't mean it in that way. My ego and pride get in the way at times; I didn't mean to hurt you. I'm sorry." His apology made me smile, even though I didn't want to. He had a different effect on me; I was myself around him whereas Leo made me want to touch him, kiss him, sending all logical thoughts out of the window.

As the thoughts of Leo entered my mind, I heard a deep growl from behind me, scaring me.

"Well, that should serve you right for entering my thoughts," I said laughing.

"Don't think about my brother when you're around me!" he growled.

"Touchy." It's not like I did it on purpose. The Kang brothers are similarly sexy when they growl, which earned me another growl, making me laugh louder.

In that moment, my skin started to get hot where Tyler's skin had touched mine.

It tingled like electricity. The sparks were visible, little bright white and blue sparks. I held my breath.

"Do you want my wolf to call you?" he whispered into my ear, sending chills down my spine.

"Uh huh!" I said turning to look at him.

"Are you sure?" He was hesitant, looking into my eyes, as though they'd give him a different answer. "Stop being a baby and show me already." In my head, I thought it was a bad idea, but I wanted to see if it was different to the cloudiness that Leo made me feel.

He closed his eyes and when he opened them they were dark, his features changed. Tyler was pretty but when his eyes darkened, he seemed dangerously sexy. He stood taller, his scent was sweeter, and he looked at me as though he would devour me in a single bite. Watching him intently, I could feel my body reacting. Instead of leaning away, I was leaning in and his eyes were drawing me closer. My heart was speeding up and my breathing escalated. He trailed his hand down my arm and I inadvertently growled at him, shocking us both. He let out a soft rumbling growl that turned my legs to jelly. He immediately reacted and lifted me up in his arms, bare chested. I was struggling to focus on anything but where his skin touched mine. He walked us further into the trees and rested my back against a trunk.

"Hold on to it," he said, looking up towards a branch above my head and I complied.

He trailed his hands down my sides, making me squirm from his touch, but not to get away, more to get closer. His hands went down my waist, hips and towards my legs. Watching me, he purposefully took his time. He lifted my legs and wrapped them around his waist. He then gently dragged his nose from my collar bone up to my neck and planted a soft kiss in the hollow area beneath my ear. I felt my legs grip him tighter as my lips released a growl which was alien to me, and my hands found themselves in his hair. Pulling hard to remove his face away from my neck, I looked into his eyes as my lips met his first. It was a hunger I couldn't explain. I bit down hard on his bottom lip, which brought the taste of blood with it. He released a growl so deep that I felt the ground shake. He then pushed me into the trunk and I pulled him towards me unable to let go. Tyler was doing his best to push me off but couldn't, something was bubbling inside me, a wild need.

"Mina, relax," he said gently. My body was not doing what I wanted it to, and there was this voice in my head that kept whispering *mine, mine, mine.* He was prying himself from me when I felt my nails dig into his skin, making him growl deeply. The need to bite this guy was making me shake in his arms. I needed him to be mine, and as I used my strength to hold on to him, I felt a sharp pain in my gum. Almost as though my mouth .was being torn apart and all I could think about was how badly I wanted to sink my teeth into his bronzed skin, which made Tyler growl even louder.

Instinctively, I lunged forward, only to be tackled to the ground. I couldn't get my senses together. I was aware of my needs for Tyler. It was real, at the forefront of everything else. I saw only Tyler. I felt hands over my eyes as I was pulled into a chest that I recognised. Clay.

"Mina, pull your shit together. Leo is here. You don't want to break out a war between the brothers. Leo will kill him. Relax." I felt as though my body was being exorcised, it was jerking in all directions. I wanted Tyler. No, I needed him.

"Clay…help…me." Unable to string my sentence together, it was clear Tyler was right; not trying to connect with whatever was in me was the better idea.

I couldn't seem to get my body into control; there was a deafening high-pitched ringing in my ears that was giving me a splitting headache and making my eyes water.

"Mina, stop fighting it and let go. The more you fight, the harder it gets." Clay's voice was soothing. I couldn't open my eyes to see where Tyler was, so I guess he had left me.

Calm down. I'm here but I can't be close to you till you calm down. I'm sorry, I didn't think it would go the way it did. Take deep breaths and focus on Clay's voice; he'll bring you back. Stop fighting it. Please.

Then it became silent. I had this urge to tear Clay apart, but I knew he was helping me. Clenching my jaws together, I tried to focus on Clay, my best friend.

"Mina, I said don't fight it. Don't be scared, I'm here. I won't leave you. So, relax and accept whatever changes you need to." Clay's voice was soothing.

Holding on to his arms to support myself, I tried to relax and let the feelings wash over me. My head started to feel cloudy and every sound became muffled. Everything hurt, and I could feel my senses slip. Great. The only thing I've learnt is that Tyler is MINE.

Clay's POV

I don't know what happened; I couldn't stop myself. I basically told her that Tyler is the right guy for her, but frankly, I've been protecting her all these years.

Yes, Tyler checked in all the time to see how she was, but he wasn't here. He didn't stop her from tripping up all the time. He didn't carry her on his back when her heels hurt too much. He didn't try to keep guys with grubby paws off her and he didn't protect her when she had night terrors.

That was all me. Mate or not.

Honestly, I didn't think I'd ever fall in love with Mina, my therian's mate. We were colleagues, friends, and somehow, she crept into my heart; her little quirks, sarcasm and clumsiness built a nest in my life. So I found myself watching her, protecting her and eventually falling in love.

I tell her we're great friends, best of friends and I'm okay not being with her, but right now, seeing her in Tyler's arms, something snapped. I don't think I can give her up.

Chapter Thirteen

"What the hell happened?" Leo's voice invaded my ears.

"We were attacked on the way here, if it wasn't for Tyler and his pack… I can't bear to think of what could've…" Clay sounded frustrated.

"My brother has his own way of doing things. Which can bring more harm than good. You should have called me." I couldn't fully grasp this rivalry between the brothers, they were family.

"Your brother does the best for Mina; he isn't selfish!" The bromance between my bestie and Tyler must have been something for him to defend the guy.

"He doesn't know what's best for Mina." Leo's voice was starting to shake a little, which wasn't a good sign. "You think you do and that's your problem. Tyler is letting Mina figure it out for herself by not trying to make this process more difficult for her. After all she's been through, she deserves to find her own way back." I guess I needed to make a dramatic entrance before the tension got physical. I don't know why I'm exhausted this morning, or how I got home to be honest.

"My ears are burning, whatchu boys talking about?" I said, stretching as far as my body would reach and then shaking it off.

"Mina, you okay?" Clay asked, concerned.

"I'm okay love and thank you for what you did, I wouldn't have been able to get through it without you." I said, vaguely remembering what happened on our way back yesterday, thankful that we had help from Tyler and his pack.

I can see Leo watching me with his face screwed up a little.

"What's wrong?" I asked, walking towards him.

"You have your guard up." He looked at me through squinted eyes.

"Obviously, I was almost attacked by some crazed guys." He walked around me as though looking for something. "No, what I mean is you're blocking my lion. What's wrong? What happened to you yesterday?" I'm blocking his spirit animal, the part of him that appeals to my senses, my cheeks flush. Remembering parts of Clay's conversation, it's weirdly all in pockets of information, rather than a linear account of everything that happened. "How can I block something I don't know?" I replied, hoping that he doesn't realise I'm flustered. I could see Clay smirking, and as our eyes met, he showed me the thumbs up with some horrendous dancing skills.

"Tell me exactly what happened yesterday!"

"Leo, I don't even understand what happened yesterday…some guys in dresses or cloaks tried to attack me for being involved with you. My life has been turned upside down. The only person giving me stability is Clay. So, stop being an idiot and help me protect myself; I didn't walk myself in here to die." I was watching Leo's face flicker with different emotions, which was interrupted by Clay.

"Mina, you didn't walk in here. I carried you here."

I had to throw Clay a dirty look. He wasn't getting what I was trying to say.

"What I meant is that I've come back here to help, not die. So, tell me what I need to do." Leo just stared at me blankly, and Clay seemed to be deep in thought.

"We need you to be out in the public eye and get you defence training," Clay answered after a couple of minutes.

"What do you mean by 'out'?" Clay just walked towards me.

"Mina, you need to be in the public eye; you need to be way up there, so if anything were to happen you'd have eyes everywhere." He pulled out his phone and sent a message.

"She doesn't need to go public. I can protect her." Leo spoke up.

"Leo, you've not been doing such a great job. The best thing for Mina would be to tap into Tyler's and River's fan bases to give her some cover before she creates her own. That is the best way to protect her, by keeping her in the public eye. No one will try to attack her if there are eyes on her, always." I could see where Clay was going with this but I'm a private person. I don't know how to be public, and if I was, I'd make an idiot out of myself by saying or doing something wrong.

"I know what's best and I'm not going to put her in the public eye," Leo stated.

"LOL! You're not going to put me in the public eye?" I said, pointing at myself a little more dramatically than I would have liked, but oh well.

"Leo, you don't have a say in my life!" I don't know why he tries to control everything.

"It came out wrong, I just meant it's a bad idea." This isn't the first time and it feels like a habit.

"I trust Clay, so I'd like to go with what he's suggesting till I think different." Clay winked at me as Leo made his way towards us.

"I'm sorry. I will try and trust your choices and not over step my boundaries," Leo said as he wrapped his arms around my shoulders.

I missed seeing Clay's face, but I can imagine it. He walked off pulling out his phone.

"Leo, I know you mean well, but you can't keep trying to control everything in my life. I can't live like that and, quite frankly, it's putting distance between us." I have to fight my way forward. I'm a therianthrope; a good one, I hope. I can't afford to sit back and let people fight my battles. I need to be ready for this.

"I understand," Leo said, holding my face, and I could feel him inching towards my lips. Even though his touch was clouding my senses, I couldn't. Not till I'd figured it all out. I stepped out of his embrace quickly.

"I'll see you later. I need to get ready for classes and see where Clay has gone and what the plan is."

"Wait… When you saw Tyler yesterday, did you catch up?" He was fishing for information. I didn't take Leo as the insecure type.

"It wasn't really the right setting for a catch up; we spoke about the past. He said we were close. I have to let you know, Tyler can be pretty annoying sometimes, but I guess that's a genetic thing between you two." I can recall snippets of Tyler too. He walked away in a huff after overhearing my thoughts about privacy, but that wasn't my fault. He shouldn't have read my mind.

As I approached, Clay put his phone back in his pocket and handed me a hot coffee and cheese bagel.

"Done canoodling?" his question made me laugh out loud.

"You just said canoodling in a serious voice." He just pushed me lightly, holding my arm so that I didn't fall on my face.

"Come on, let's get you to class; it's going to be a long day," he said, dragging me through the corridors.

The lessons weren't a big deal. I mean sure it was a lot of information to take in, but Clay and I spent the first few days sitting at the back corner of the classes with as little interaction as possible. We were the oldest ones, so it was lucky that we didn't stick out much.

Everything was weirdly interesting apart from the physical aspects. I genuinely sucked at physical activity. My fitness levels were beyond pathetic and, I really needed to work on the wheezing after classes. I wanted to learn more and be better at fitting in. I made a few friends who helped Clay and me through the class content. There was Sebastian Riz, who was an art major, and helped both Clay and I come out of our shells. He was tall, dark and handsome, probably the next big thing. He said, "If you get over the fear of looking silly, then nothing can affect you, so go out there and do something outrageous where people will laugh at you and then you'll be fine."

It was my worst nightmare, having people looking at me and laughing, but he was right. After further pep talks from Sebastian, I went out with my eyes closed and decided to try out some tone-deaf singing as Clay stood at my side dancing; it was worlds away from his artist self. He thought he'd be creating magnificent art, not dancing. Afterwards, we were given a round of applause by the students who came up to us to congratulate us on our courage, explaining that it always gets easier.

Emilia Rose was our mentor for etiquette and common manner lessons; she was aristocratic. We had met before. She was a fan of River. A blue-eyed, brown-haired, rosy-cheeked young woman, she was the definition of an English rose. She laughed so brightly that for a minute you forgot she was way above your status in society, unlike us 'common folk', as she stated so simply. She told me that "Where you come from has nothing to do with where you're going. Keep that in mind, it's all an act. Changing your mannerisms can make you a different person altogether". But do I want to be a different person? It took me twenty-five years to love who I am today; why do I need to change? I could tell that Clay liked Emilia and vice versa. I did feel a tinge of jealousy but got over it quickly when he looked over at me from time to time.

For meditation, Chi and spirit unification, we had a completely chilled-out guy called Wang Zi. He was tall and thin with broad shoulders and, if he was any more laidback he'd be asleep. I loved this class the most. It's all about self-realisation and appreciating who you are and what you bring to the world. We practiced Chi and breathing techniques and I loved every minute. The day was always packed with lessons and physical activity and it became the highlight of every evening. Clay didn't take as much away from it as I did, as he preferred strenuous activity.

Then there was Ziyad Bakari, who was so into languages he kept swapping between French, Spanish and English, which became a little frustrating, as it was difficult to keep up. He was probably the one guy I felt comfortable to look at. He was cute but not so much that you'd stare a hole into his face and, the youngest at nineteen. He tried his best to teach us languages, but it felt rushed and I had to remind him that we needed to learn the basics before we jumped into conversations. But he only replied with, "No English, try Spanish or French. It doesn't matter if you get it wrong, practice makes perfect." To which Clay and I rolled our eyes. He just didn't get it.

Finally, our defence and resistance guy was Hahona Turei. I still struggle to say his name, but he was totally sweet about it and I remembered him taking a picture with River. He was more our age, at twenty-three. One look at him and you'd know he worked hard on his defence training and all aspects of physical activity. He had a full arm of intricate tribal tats that I kept glancing at in awe—they were beautiful. He worked us like crazy though and kept telling me to put more effort into my training. Like seriously, I don't work out at all. It's not something I'm proud of but it's just not in me to do it; by the end of his sessions, I was always aching and close to a heart attack not looking forward to waking up with cramps the following day. Even Clay struggled but Hahona kept us at it.

After the first few weeks, I realised that the tutors for the classes were interchangeable. It seemed that certain topics were taught by specific tutors, they tended to set the topic of the lesson and then let you figure it all out yourself and, you could always contact them if need be. Most of the classes were led by the top students like our mentors. Our group clicked for more than one reason and we all became fast friends. It was great sitting around the tables at meal times and eating with everyone. Each day, I felt more like I belonged and having River and Clay there made it even more special. Caaliyah also joined us at times. Initially, she was avoided as she was a shadow, but soon it didn't matter. Good food and conversations ruled our table and Caaliyah was so knowledgeable, we pretty much saw her as one of us, without the shadow label. That didn't go down well with all of the other students. We saw a lot of side glances and heard whispers behind our backs about us not understanding rank. But none of that mattered to us; well, it didn't feel like it did as we were in our own happy bubble.

I rarely got to see Tyler after that day, even though I noticed him in classes sometimes. He was off on some K-pop tour with his members. I saw Angelico from time to time; he was the sweetest, giving me updates on Tyler's whereabouts. I told him there was no need, but he said it was an excuse to see his 'Luna', which I appreciated. I got to see the other wolves too, who were all willing to give me pointers on my lesson subjects. Their patience with me was outstanding.

Leo and I were on friendly terms but that was it, no weird feelings or thoughts, which helped me to better focus on my studies. He was busy working on ensuring that he secured his spot on the throne. He was determined to prove to me and the Royal circle that I was the right girl for the job, but I didn't see it.

Things changed for me again one night. We all met on the rooftop of the girl's wing with blankets and hot chocolate just to catch up; it was becoming a habit. We sat around a makeshift fire and decided to talk about our spirit animals. Clay and I went first as we didn't have much to share at that moment, which was fine by them.

They reassured us that it would come soon, you just needed something significant to happen, that triggers the change. River showed off some of her scales as she told us she was a sea serpent. They glistened in the moonlight and the guys stared at her face as she had a purplish glow.

Then they all took turns. Sebastian was a mountain gorilla who stood on strong, muscular gorilla arms, which looked odd with his human body. Emilia changed the colouring of her face to match the markings of her fallow deer spirit. Wang Zi showed off his tiger fangs. Hahona let out a magnificent Jaguar roar and let his eyes reflect the moonlight and, Ziyad replaced his nose with his rhino horn. We were all different, yet equally the same. We were therians finding our place in the world. The oddest bunch of friends, harbouring a non-spirit without knowing. I did feel bad about lying to them, but I needed Clay.

We carried on talking and everyone told us about the hardships of turning and the pain and responsibility it came with. We talked about mates, the girls more animatedly than the guys. That's when Emilia told us she had found her mate. I looked over at Clay to make sure he was okay. He just stood and came to sit behind me, wrapping his arms around me to keep me warm. Hahona's workouts were working on him too. I had lost a few pounds, but Clay's biceps were a lot larger than I remembered. I blushed at my thought.

Emilia told us about her mate. She said she was disgusted by him initially and became so traumatised when she realised who he was, she previously had such hateful thoughts towards him, and put it down to social normalisation. Her mate was a hybrid, Elk and Stallion named Yousef Mahmud. She was distraught that they were so different, even if their spirit animals kind of belonged to the same species; she was wary that their upbringing was different as he wasn't a full blood cervidae and, she was a little scared of his views, including his human way of life and what he expected. It turned out that all he wanted was to protect her with all he had. She laughed, saying his gentle nature was a little too placid for her; not the usual type of guy she fell for, but apparently, she couldn't compare him to any other guy. He made her feel whole and nothing else mattered. Even her family were struggling to accept him, as he didn't fit their ideal of a pure blood and now she was struggling to not choose between her mate and her family.

As she told her story, I felt a twinge of pain in my heart.

At the end of the night, Clay walked me to the doors of the girls' wing. Caaliyah and River had something to do, so I was walking to my room by myself when I saw Jesse. At first, I thought I was seeing things and did a double take. He was with Nathaniel. Did they know each other? Had Jesse come looking for me? As I opened my mouth to call out for him, a hand cut off the sound. I kicked and struggled. Now was not the time to get kidnapped, I thought as I was pulled into the shadows of one of the murals.

"Stop kicking, it's me." Tyler's voice soothed my fear.

"You idiot! Do you take pleasure in scaring me?" I hissed.

"Yes, I actually do," he said, smirking as he backed me further into the darkness.

"That's someone I know, I need to speak to him." I had to know why Jesse was here.

"You know the guy with Nathaniel?" he questioned. I couldn't really see his face, but I heard a little anger. "Yes, that's Jesse, my ex. I think he's here looking for me." I felt the growl rumbling in his body, it sent shivers through me. He silenced himself against my neck and I felt the vibrations. Thoughts of Jesse left my mind as I pulled Tyler closer and my hand crept up his shirt, but he stopped me. The sting of embarrassment was something I needed to get used to. I didn't know what had come over me or why I had reacted so forwardly to his growl. It was natural; the sound connected me to him.

"Not here." His words resonated within me. I can't explain the rush they had on me. His hands were still on mine, but his body was a lot closer, towering over me.

"Mina, don't look at me like that, you're not making this easy on me." Making what easy?

"Okay, I'll go back to my room," I said, walking away.

"Wait," he pulled me back towards him and, as we collided, I remembered the moment in the forest and it all rushed back.

Bloodmoon's POV

She is not ready, how many times can I block her memories before she breaks. I can't let her come to harm, or let our mate get hurt in the process of her change.

Every time Tyler is close, I can feel myself at the surface, but she's still weak and afraid, blocking her mind and energy. She needs to sort that out and soon or when the change happens, we will have no control and people will get hurt.

I will not let that be Tyler.

Chapter Fourteen

I woke up with the worst headache; Clay was waiting as patiently as he could. We were late and needed to rush to get to class. At one point Clay lifted me into the air and started running.

I must admit, today I felt a little weird. My skin had this weird static sensation and I can't figure out why. Unfortunately, I had to skip breakfast, but as soon as my eyes landed on Ziyad's cheese toasty, my stomach rumbled. He begrudgingly passed me half his toasty as Clay laughed.

"It's better to feed her than let her hungry monster out. I learnt the hard way and now I just continuously feed her." Ziyad just responded in French and I couldn't tell if his reply was nice or not.

The day went okay but I couldn't get over the weird feeling in the pit of my stomach. I couldn't figure out what had been going on with me recently.

I decided to learn Spanish as one of my languages. It had been a while now and I was still getting to grips with the basics. After class, Ziyad and Clay went to get food before the next lesson. Thankfully, they're a lot faster on their feet than me, so I just made my way to the next class. Today's topic is dance. I just hope I make it through without crushing anyone's toes.

I was met at the door by Sebastian, who was talking to a young girl with blonde bouncy curls. It seemed that I interrupted their conversation as Sebastian gripped me in a gorilla hug. The blue eyes of the girl gave me a disgruntled look and I smacked him to let go, which didn't work till a guy reached over me and pushed him off.

"This is class, not a make out session," Tyler's voice sent tingles up my spine.

"We weren't making out," I replied as the blue-eyed girl grinned at me.

"Move it, class starts soon." He shoved past us like we had done something wrong.

"What's up his…" Sebastian nudged me to be quiet and I realised I'd spoken too loud, as everyone was staring, including Tyler. Embarrassed, I tried to hide behind Sebastian and peek. Tyler's eyes were still on me. Soon everyone crowded around the tutor and Tyler. I wasn't really feeling the need to join them. Only Clay turned up with food and coerced me into paying attention. Who can reject a freshly baked cinnamon roll? It turned out the lesson today wasn't dancing, it was on 'stage presence and personality' and Tyler was the guest tutor, along with 'Zero', his group. The entire class went crazy. Girls were crying and, I was at a loss for words over the commotion. Six other guys came into the room and the phones were out, snapping away. The guys were signing clothes, bags, paper and even bare skin. Tyler had girls around him and it irked me. I don't know why, but I avoided the crowd and watched on from a distance. All seven were matching with similar styles—tight jeans and loose tops. They all wore some sort of makeup and accessories to the max.

I had to contain a growl when I saw a girl rubbing Tyler's abdomen. Like seriously? He caught my eye and smirked, so I decided to get some distance and sat next to Clay and Sebastian, who were avoiding the chaos.

"You okay, bestie?" Clay asked.

"Yes, why wouldn't I be?" I replied, almost biting his head off. I put it down to hormones of the upcoming cycle. "So, what's the deal? Why are they going crazy over there?" I asked Sebastian, who just looked at me like I'd got out from under a rock.

"That's Zero, one of the largest international boy groups in the world, their fan bases are literally global. Have you not heard of the Korean wave? It's sweeping through every country. Girls dream to be with them and guys dream to be them. They're some of the best Clandestanites out there." He looked offended.

"Erm, I don't think they're big where we live," I said, trying to sound apologetic. I realised I might need to brush up on the other Clandestanites who were successful, or at least try my hand at being more social.

"You guys not fans?" One of the Zero guys had somehow made his way to us. He had bright red hair and thick liner.

I just looked at Clay for help, not wanting to make a further fool of myself by saying something wrong.

"It's not that, we're just new and haven't really had time to adjust," he said, smiling at the stranger.

"Okay cool, you can call me Romeo, I'm the lead rapper in the group," he said, extending his hand out to us all.

"The guy with the long hair is Ty," he said pointing at Tyler, who was looking over at us somewhat annoyed. "The one with the bandana is Mike, the low pants is Jeonghoon, the guy with the ripped shirt showing off is Zixu, the blue hair is Min and, finally, the kiddie looking one is Taeyong," I doubt I'd remember any of their names other than Tyler.

"You guys should come and check us out, we're holding a show on the grounds in a few days. I have some tickets if you want?" I was just looking at him like are you serious?

Before I could make up any excuse, Sebastian snatched them out of Romeo's hand, making him laugh. "You guys better start walking back up to the group as we are doing a stage presence session. Ty's known to be hot-headed when people waste his time." With that he was up and we started to follow him. I asked Sebastian what his issue with the tickets was and he smiled sheepishly.

"I'm not a crazy fan, but do you know how expensive it is to go to a Zero concert. It sells out within seconds and they're pretty good. Plus, I think it would be a good experience for you guys. He's given us enough tickets for the others too. Group date!" he said, and everyone just turned to glare at us.

The lesson itself was weird to say the least. Each of the guys showed us why they worked as part of the group and how they had different components they brought to the whole package, creating a synergy. Romeo was the lead rapper, so he was vocally charismatic; his voice was so unique and gravelly that even I could pick it from a group of people. Mike was the funny guy, the one who told all the embarrassing stories about the rest of the members. He was also the one who went on televised shows to promote the group. Jeonghoon was the lead dancer. His moves were incredible and, he hit every beat, including ones I couldn't even hear. Zixu was the 'visual', like they weren't all good looking, everyone wanted a piece of him, male or female, and I could see why; light blue eyes and pale skin with bright pink lips. He also had perfectly straight teeth. Min was the one who was sensible with manners. He was polite and took time to speak with all his fans, I liked him the most, his mannerisms were ones you don't get to see every day, so down to earth and genuine. Taeyong was the maknae (baby) of the group. He was filled with energy; it was his responsibility to cheer everyone up, like that would be easy with someone like Tyler in the group. Finally, Tyler was the leader. His presence was dominating, even when standing he exuded power and something far out of reach.

We were eventually divided into groups and given a task of bringing something different to it. I was lucky I had Sebastian and Clay in my group, as well as some other faces that I hadn't worked with before. The girl with the bouncy curls was there too. She placed herself between Clay and Sebastian, marking her spot. Going around the group, we all had to decide what we had to offer. Clay was selected as the visual obviously, as the rest of the group consisted of females that he had previously interacted with. Sebastian was selected as the funny guy, the actor who could change and adapt to any situation, and we needed someone like that to bring up the dynamic of the group.

Curls was the maknae, the ball of energy. Then there was a rapper, a dancer and a main vocalist, which left me. Everyone looked at me, waiting for me to show some sort of talent and I couldn't; I had nothing. Their eyes were fixed on me and I felt the discomfort growing. How do I fit into this group? I barely compare in talent. I didn't want to have some sort of emotional breakdown, but the scrutiny was getting to me. Clay and Sebastian were both trying to encourage me with smiles, but it wasn't working. I needed a minute. Curls smirked and I realised she was not really the friendly type.

I watched all the groups from a distance and saw they all had something. I didn't have any talent and my personality wasn't big, so what did I have? I didn't want to embarrass myself in front of everyone and definitely not Tyler. I wished River or Leo would turn up; they both knew how to make me feel good about myself. All the groups were taking to the stage to present themselves and I was just going to ruin it for my team. My heart started to race, and I could feel my eyes stinging. What do I do?

Don't second guess yourself, you're the Luna of the world's largest wolf pack. Do you not understand the power that you possess? When you enter the room, I can't take my eyes off you. You make me feel things that no woman has and you're not even mine. Tyler's voice entered my mind and I forgot that he could hear my thoughts. His voice sent tingles through me and his words did something more.

Good, I'm glad they do something more; do you want to know what you do to me? His words made me more nervous, was he purposefully trying to make me fail? I let my eyes search the groups for him and when they landed on his, I felt the rush. His eyes were piercing as he scanned me feet up, and I watched as his eyes darkened. A guttural sound then escaped my lips, thankfully only Clay and Sebastian were close enough to hear.

They turned to look at me in shock.

Careful love, you're tempting me! What does that even mean? Can you get out of my head, Tyler?

Is that what you really want? Do you not remember last night?

What happened last night? Hello? There was radio silence. My mind, however, was filled with images of us and I remembered, his hands, my skin, my hands, his skin, his lips and I looked at him again. He balled his hands into fists and he let out a growl, scaring everyone. Zero surrounded him and I saw Romeo say something, which made him visibly relax. I understood, and I felt different, I don't need to make an impression on anyone but me. I was so worried about being perfect and acceptable that I was losing my individual identity. I had always struggled to connect to my own sensuality and womanliness as I was cautious of the image I presented, but why do I have to caution myself for the thoughts of others?

It was our turn to go on the makeshift stage one by one. They all did their bit, introducing themselves and what they had to offer. I looked down at myself and realised I needed to change. As Curls was doing her bit, I called Clay over. He was wearing a white dress shirt with a leather jacket. I needed his shirt. Quickly undoing my dress, I asked Clay for his shirt. He looked bewildered that I was changing in front of him. I had mix matched underwear, a nice blue crop and some black boxers. Luckily, no one would see the boxers. Clay was trying to stop me from changing and I asked him to trust me. He complied and reluctantly took off his shirt, before handing it to me.

I unscrewed my water bottle and poured it all over my hair. I was going for the shock value, regardless of the embarrassment, I will push through it. As no one would ever imagine 'timid Mina' would appear in just a dress shirt. I checked my make-up and freshened up where I needed to. As I heard my name being called I inhaled and walked on tiptoes. This was it. I tried to straighten my back and elongate my arms and legs, continuously reminding myself I was a Luna and that Tyler and I kissed—the guy out of everyone else's reach made out with me last night. The tingles on my skin were of a delicious nature, when I remembered his exact words, "Use me and only me!" Tyler didn't like the idea of me having Leo and now Jesse back in my life. I felt sexy and confident as I walked out. My group did a double take and everyone else cheered as I walked on. I didn't say a word, just flicked my hair once and locked eyes with Tyler. I could tell he wasn't happy with my decision as the Zero boys were holding him back.

You better go behind the screen and get some clothes back on.

I don't know why but his words made me smile. I heard his growls in my mind too, they were underlined with annoyance. After our applause, I went to change. Curls decide to barge past me, knocking me over. I felt arms around me before I hit the ground. Looking up, my eyes met with Tyler's dark ones, and his grip on me tightened. He let me stand and then stood there whilst I changed, which was strangely empowering. There's something between us and I need to figure out what because it's driving me crazy.

"Your teasing could lead to trouble; do you want trouble, Mina?" he whispered behind my ear, making me freeze on the spot. Clay came up behind us, asking for his shirt and Tyler walked away.

Everything changed for me after the stage presence day. Students took notice in a good way. Before it had been all weird comments about how Clay and I were outsiders, but now they wanted to be friends. I, however, didn't need any more. I was good with the ones who became my friends before my show-and-tell session. They knew the real me and chose to be my friend without the façade.

The days started to get longer, and I was more focused on studying—not out of choice, mind you. It was more because I needed to block out thoughts of Tyler. I was starting to daydream about this guy and it was straining my friendship with Leo. We fell out an unbelievable amount of times as he kept questioning about my relationship with Tyler, even though nothing had happened except that kiss. Not that I wanted to divulge that information to Leo, not after I knew that he'd taken advantage of my vulnerability. That first kiss, the moment we met still needed to be discussed, he needs to know how wrong it was.

I woke up late again after tossing and turning all night. Breakfast on the go is the worst thing for me. Trying to eat as fast as possible, I followed Clay's lead and we ended up in a room that had *Languages, History and Culture Studies Group A* on the door, we had finally worked all the way up from group D. Clay took us up to the back where there were two seats next to each other. I saw the other 'students' look at us like we were aliens. They were kids not much older than nineteen.

"Ahem… You're in my seat," said a familiar young girl with round blue eyes and blonde bouncy curls. She was looking at me intently, willing me out of her seat.

"Claudia, stop lying, we don't have assigned seats." A young lad winked at me from the front, making me laugh, the same one from Nathaniel's waiting area all those months ago.

"It's fine, I'll move, don't worry." I didn't want to create an even worse time for myself, especially with a teen. Like going .back to school wasn't bad enough.

I got up to leave and Clay followed, only to be pulled back by Claudia.

"You don't need to leave, there's room for you." She fluttered her lashes at him. I'm so used to Clay being hit on that it seemed normal.

"Erm. Listen, kid, you're not my type; try dating guys your own age," Clay replied as he pried her fingers off him. The girl's got a good grip, I have to give her that. She then shot me a glaring look, changing her face from a friendly one to some creepy serial killer thing. I guess she was really into Clay, no wonder she sat with him during our stage presence session.

"FYI we're not together... so no need to give me the daggers," I said, and her face softened.

"I can't take you anywhere. Why did you have to be mean? Normally you take it in your stride," I muttered to Clay as we walked to the front. Best seats in the house.

"If you hadn't noticed, I've not been with any girls recently. I'm not looking to get involved." I tried not to laugh.

"Casanova of the modern world has sworn off girls?" I say playfully shoving him and tripping over my own feet. "I have my hands full with you," he replied as he caught me before I face planted the chair. His eyes had this weird piercing look that made me drop the subject.

As we sat down, I heard the whispers settle and everyone take their seat. To my surprise, I saw Cairo at the front of the class and felt my heart sink. His eyes zeroed in on me and there was a faint glimmer of a smirk that I wanted to slap off his face.

"Class welcome, we are introducing a couple of new students to this group, please support them where necessary. Would you please stand up and introduce yourselves?" He gestured at Clay and me.

"My name is Alexander Clayton," Clay went first and sat down.

"My name is Mina Michaels," I told the group, but before I could even sit down, Cairo had asked me a question.

"Miss Michaels, what is your ethnicity?" The question threw me.

"I don't understand. I was born and bred in England and I was adopted."

"Are you white, like Mr. Clayton?" he pressed.

"I don't think so; like I said, I was adopted." I knew he was trying to make me uncomfortable as all of the kids now started to focus on me. I felt my hands start to clam up.

"I don't see how that is relevant?" I could feel the heat off Clay, who always gets defensive whenever he feels I am being backed into a corner.

"You don't care what blood courses through your veins?" he questioned.

"Not really, unless the blood in my veins affects who I am as a person," I replied, thinking that he could take his stinking attitude elsewhere.

"The blood in your veins gives you your identity, Miss Michaels. Your ethnicity allows you to connect with people like yourself, it helps you understand your own history and culture. Without it, who are you really?" I could see his point, but he didn't need to call me out on my first day in a new group; I worked hard to move up.

"Yes, it does, you're right, but so does common decency and respect for those around me. I can connect with love and kindness too. I may not know what my ethnic background is, but I was raised by two good, loving parents and yes, my skin is different to theirs, but they are still my parents. Unless you have some issue with the colour of people's skin, can I sit down?" My comments were met with echoing oohs from the kids around me. The guy who previously winked at me gave me a thumbs up from behind his seat. I needed to remember to catch his name.

"You may sit!" He looked shocked by my comments, as everyone turned to look at the pompous prince.

The rest of the lesson dragged. Cairo insisted on hovering around me which earned him a few grunts from Clay. I had to hold him down in his seat so that he didn't draw any more attention to us. Cairo gave Clay and me some huge books to read through, and set us tasks as to which languages we wanted to learn. Honestly, there were so many to choose from. He also gave us a thick ancient book covered in rustic art and gold writing called *Therian the Memoir*. By thick, I mean it was as wide as my thigh. How are we expected to carry that? Deciding to flick through it, I find that the pages are blank.

"Are we creating our own memoir?" I asked. The class erupted into laughter, making me squirm a little.

"No, these hold the ancestry of our own bloodline," said the cute kid in front.

"Oh…" I don't know what else to say without drawing further attention. I could see Cairo's smugness from the corner of my eye and my anger bubbled. He wasn't going to make this any easier for me.

"Pssst…" I kick the cute kid's chair. As he turned towards me, he winked again and smiled.

"Miss me already?" he said laughing.

"Sure… What's your name, ladies' man?" I said smiling.

"Theodore Browne at your service," he replied bowing playfully in his chair. I couldn't help but laugh. I could get used to more friendly people. I could feel Clay's glare from the side.

"Okay, do you prefer Theo or Teddy?" I asked, looking at this boy's large brown eyes.

"Everyone calls me Theo, but I can be your teddy?" making me laugh a little too loud.

"Miss Michaels, do you have something to share with us?" Cairo shouted across the room.

"No, sorry…" I whispered.

"Nice try Theo, can you tell me why my book is blank?" I said, leaning over so as to not get the attention of Cairo again.

"You need to use your own blood on it. The memoirs have some sort of enchanted paper that can only be activated by blood. It's so that each individual's skills and history is secret to them, unless they want to share them. By the way, you smell lovely. What is it?" I have to put blood on a book to read it.

"Wild Ashes, it's handmade by yours truly," I smiled at him and he mirrored my smile. He started to lean further in towards me, only to be smacked on the forehead by Clay, which shocked us all.

"Miss Michaels, you may leave and sit outside the room," said Cairo, pulling me up when he saw it wasn't me.

"It wasn't her Cairo…" Theo tried to speak, only to be interrupted.

"I will see you at the end." I gave Clay daggers as I got up and Theo weakly smiled as I left the room and plonked myself on the bench outside.

I wasn't going to hang around for something I didn't do. Plus, the Zero performance was on tonight and I needed to work on my appearance. Not that I was fan girling over them; I just wanted to capture Tyler's attention. He'd been avoiding me recently and I was not having it. There was something between us and I needed to know what.

Cairo's POV

A lot of whispers have been going around about Mina. She's no longer the new girl everyone avoided and has somehow built a unique set of friends, all different with an alliance to her. None of them were friends before Mina came on the scene. They are even accepting Shadows into their circle, how is that possible?

She's somehow placed herself on the radar of the rogues and the McGuire's by hanging around the Kangs, not exactly a good thing for her. Those brothers take trouble wherever they go and right now she's got herself right in the middle.

My father always told me that there will be a time when the weak will stand strong and it will be due to love and kindness, not power. I wondered if this would be the time. As a Prince, I have had my fair share of hardships. My father has been ill and my mother struggles to keep her place on the throne till either Hameed or I am ready. This is always a cause for arguments.

I don't want to rule with fear, as fear only goes so far. I need to have the respect that my father had, and Mina seems to get that without being forceful. I need to know her.

Chapter Fifteen

When I got to my room, River and Caaliyah were waiting. Emilia followed a few minutes later and we all proceeded to get ready for the night's activities. I ended up in a beautiful red flowing gown that belonged to River. I would never normally wear a colour so bright, but I needed something he would see straight away.

"Red, huh? And I didn't even need to force it on you. Something you want to share with the rest of the group?" River eyed me weirdly, which piqued the interest of the other two girls, as suddenly they were around me, their eyes wide, ears open.

"Noo…" I brushed them away but the heat in my cheeks gave me away.

"You're blushing, Mina," Caaliyah pointed out and I pulled back a scowl.

"Is it Leo?" River asked. She still believed he was my mate. I didn't want to correct her without confirming my thoughts first and I've not felt a pull towards Leo since I met Tyler.

"Stop, it's nothing like that," I said, trying to keep my face blank so as to not react to any of the other names they threw my way.

"Is it any of the other boys? I mean I do think they're good-looking, especially Hahona; even the guys find him attractive." River annoyingly started to make kissing noises as she held up a pillow to her face, and here I was thinking we were grown women, but there's always one weirdo in a group, I suppose.

"I know who it is; it's so obvious, girls. I don't see how you haven't noticed. I noticed all the little things after I met Yousef. I've caught him staring at her, when she's not watching, like he's always in awe of her presence. Yousef looks at me that way too. I can't believe it took you this long to figure it out, Mina." My heart was racing, how did Emilia figure it out and does Tyler really look at me like that? Every time I caught his eye, he always looks annoyed or has that deliciously dangerous look that makes my heart beat a little faster.

"I don't know what YOU'RE talking about," I said, and all the girls laughed because of my overreaction. "See, I told you. It's amazing you found each other even before you knew what you both were. The strongest loves always start with friendship. Clay is so good to you." Wait what? Clay? She thinks I'm into Clay? I didn't even deny it as it was a shock. I know how Clay feels, he told me, but I always took it with a pinch of salt. He's my best friend and I don't want anything clouding our friendship; he's like family.

At that moment, all the lads walked through the door, all animated as there was a new face among them. He was tall and slim with a good amount of stubble. It was clear to us who he was. As he entered the room, his eyes were transfixed on Emilia. Yousef. The guys did a great job styling themselves, they were all in dark jeans and lace-up boots in all shades. Sebastian and Ziyad were in dress shirts, their hair styled in parted side quiffs. Hahona had on a black sleeveless top, showing off his bulging biceps and tattoo, his hair falling at his shoulders. Wang Zi was dressed all in white. He could probably fit into Zero based on his style, no issues. He wore the white on white ensemble pretty dang well, although his drop crotch jeans did look a tad bit tight in my eyes. Clay was in a loose red knit jumper, his hair falling over his eyes as usual. I swear we didn't coordinate. When I looked up at him his eyes looked somewhat glazed, and he had the weirdest smile, which left the girls in hysterics and the guys a little confused. At this point, I was the same colour as my dress.

"Are we going or what?" I huffed.

"You look really nice, Mina," Clay said, only to be met with more howls of laughter. This is going to be a long night. We made our way to an out building a short walk away from Clandestine. The roof was open, and it was completely packed. Clay ensured his arms were up at either side of me as he walked behind me to block people from walking into me. The girls kept glancing over, making weird faces, and Hahona caught on. He raised his brows questioningly at me.

"Don't start, they're overthinking it. We are friends!" I whispered a little too aggressively and he held his hands up before moving people out of our path as politely as he could. We were getting hostile stares, myself included, from some of the females. The girls from all of our classes made small talk as we walked through the crowd to get closer to the stage, and along the way, River was hounded for selfies, which made me question how big her role was at Clandestine.

Everything was dimly lit, and the night sky was littered with stars. The stage was circular, somewhat reminding me of Shakespeare's Globe Theatre. The guys got us a lot closer to the stage than we would have anticipated, which was great as I thought Tyler wouldn't be able to miss me now. Clay had his arm around me just in case I was cold, as he put it, and the girls just played up to it. I was a little distracted as I had an uneasy feeling of being watched, but then again, most people were looking at us all. Our group was blended with no hierarchy, which rubbed a few people up the wrong way, while others were intrigued by how well we all got along. Hahona had both Sebastian and Ziyad in a headlock and Wang Zi just looked embarrassed to be around them. He started to walk towards me when the crowd suddenly erupted, and the stage lit up.

Zero were standing a few feet away as the music started. They were all in black suits with fancy open collar shirts and matching shoes. Tyler caught my eye. His hair was a darker colour and he had it tied up with a few strands falling out, which elongated his face. He looked directly at me and smiled. I forgot that he could hear my thoughts and here I was ogling him. When he saw what I was wearing, his eyes widened and darkened. I didn't need to read his mind to understand what he was thinking as he let his eyes fall down the full length of my leg that was escaping out of the slit in the dress. His gaze made me shiver, which Clay mistook as me being cold. He pulled me closer into him and further tightened his arms around my shoulders. Tyler noticed immediately and his face hardened, so I escaped Clay's arms and walked over to River, who was dancing away.

Yousef held Emilia's hand as she danced with us, keeping his eyes firmly on her. On the other side, Caaliyah had her eyes on the group of guys behind us. I turned to see that she had her eyes on Cairo. I mean Cairo, really? Of all the gorgeous guys present, he catches her attention. To be honest, I wanted to go over and smack him in the face but thought better of it. As I cleared my throat, she jumped up and she realised I had caught her. She looked at her feet, then at River and the rest of us, to see who else saw. She then made a pleading face at me to which I raised my brow and shrugged. I would let her squirm a little bit; she had thoroughly enjoyed teasing me just minutes before. My eyes scanned the crowd around us and I saw Wang Zi do the same, had he felt that we were being watched too?

The set that Zero played was amazing, even though I hardly understood a word they sang and rapped. The atmosphere was electric. They danced for seventy percent of their performance and thirty percent were ballads, which were used as resting points, I guess. I purposefully avoided Tyler's eyes throughout the performances. Romeo gave me a shout out, so I threw him my best smile and he reciprocated with a heart. I have to say I didn't think it would have been as exhilarating as it was, everyone was buzzing. The show was at its climax and the final performance was a soft, soothing ballad called 'Sarang' with Tyler taking the lead. Who knew the boy could sing? I made the mistake of looking at him, as his eyes were fixated on me, and I couldn't remove my gaze from him. By the end of it, my legs were all jelly and my cheeks hot.

I used my palms to cool them down as the stage released fireworks into the sky and everyone cheered *Zero! Zero! Zero!* I didn't want to own up to it, but I felt my inner fan girl trying to escape. I will be downloading their music and putting the playlist on loop.

It wasn't until the lights dimmed down again that I felt a weird prickle at the back of my neck. I was being watched, but by who? I scanned the crowd, and no one stood out. I clung to River, so I wouldn't break away from the group. The night sky was chillier and quiet. Everyone had rushed back and here we were strolling. I didn't want to break the mood, so I turned to Hahona.

"I feel weird," I whispered to him.

"What do you mean?" he said, checking my pulse.

"I'm not ill. We're being watched." Hahona is the sweetest, mellowest guy I have met. He works a lot with herbs and organic medicine. His mother taught him that the Earth offers a cure for illnesses if you look for them properly. He's somewhat a healer.

"By who? Where?" His posture changed, and he called the boys to gather around us. Wang Zi took the lead. He stepped in front of us all and told us to be quiet; he could hear something. He whispered something to the rest of the guys and I found myself in the centre with the rest of the girls, as the boys circled around us as a shield. Caaliyah joined them, there was no way she would step back and be protected. She was River's Shadow; her job was to protect. I felt somewhat inadequate, finding myself in trouble again and not being able to do anything. Out of the shadows came a few Clandestine students we'd seen; the Pierce triplets, Curls, and a few other students who had previously shared their disdain at our circle of friends. I saw Michael, a boy who was in Cairo's class with me and Clay, who sat next to Ziyad during language sessions.

"This is wrong, you have been warned. The likes of you lot make us sick," a girl with white hair said and took a step forward, her jaws snapping. Michael pulled her back.

"What do you mean the likes of us? Girl, don't compare yourself to me," River retorted. I knew she had a temper, but I was having a hard time keeping a hold of her. I really didn't want our evening to be ruined by some silly views.

"You don't get it, do you? What you're doing is wrong. It's sickening. You don't belong together," said another lad who was standing with his arm around Angel Pierce.

"You guys have a choice to do and be whatever you want. We all had an amazing night and want to keep it that way, so if you can move out of our way, we don't want trouble," Wang Zi spoke this time, sounding calm under the circumstances.

"Unfortunately, we can't let you leave. Not yet, anyway," one lad said, and a few more students joined them; none of them had smiles. It was hard for me to believe. We were all studying and getting along all right all these months and it had taken just a group of us to become good friends to rub them up the wrong way.

How could friendship and understanding the differences we all had be wrong? The world was turning on its head, all because of our different origins.

"We aren't doing you any harm, we aren't asking to be friends with you either, so please leave us alone."

Caaliyah was trying to move us forward as she spoke, but the reaction got worse.

"How dare you speak to us when no one has addressed you? You're a mere Shadow; know your place," one of the triplets shouted and then spat in Caaliyah's face. That was the last straw.

River started to turn, and I was unable to keep a hold of her. She started to hum gently to herself and her skin began to change to scales, while her hair lengthened and spread out around her. Thankfully, her tail didn't make an appearance. She moved in front of Caaliyah and muttered something, to which Caaliyah closed her eyes and raised her arms. River's hum turned into a high-pitched screech. Caaliyah started to make circular movements with her hands, which looked a little odd, but I soon understood why. The circular moves took on a form of white and made their way up to River's mouth and gills unexpectedly appeared on either side of her lower neck. The sound of the screech reached a different level, piercing our ears painfully. It became muffled as the white clouds covered her lips.

In front of us, however, a different story was unfolding. Liv Pierce who had spat at Caaliyah became rigid, her face pale. I heard screams from the other girls around us as blood started to seep out of her mouth, eyes and ears. I knew then that I had to stop River before she did something stupid out of anger. I ran to her side only to be knocked into Wang Zi. He helped me up and told me there was a force field around River. Caaliyah's doing, obviously, so there was no way out of it. The only thing I could think of doing was standing in front of her screech. I braced myself for the same effects and watched the others behind me start to disperse out of fear. I felt the full effect of River's power as my body writhed in pain. It was such an unbearably high-pitched sound that I felt like it was clawing away at my insides.

"River!" I tried to shout but could feel no sound escape my lips.

I had only been standing in front of her for thirty seconds and knew I can't do anymore. I felt the wetness down my cheeks and ears. Thankfully, I saw the boys trying to figure something out before Clay rammed into Caaliyah, knocking her to the floor. River opened her eyes as soon as the screeching was at its optimum sound. Her eyes met with mine and she closed her mouth, before rushing to my side as my knees hit the ground.

Michael came and dragged the girl beside me away. When I saw his face, I knew he was ashamed but there was nothing he could do. He mouthed "I'm sorry". For what, I didn't know, but soon found out.

My eyes and ears hurt, and there was a burning sensation in my throat. River profusely apologised for what had happened, and I think I said it was okay. Clay's face was easy to read, as his fear was plain to see. I smiled to reassure him, but he just turned his back to me. Yousef had his arms around Emilia, and Hahona was by my side. His hands pressed on my ears and then my throat. I felt a cooling sensation and the pain eased. He then pressed his hands over my eyes, and as I felt the same cooling sensation, something else caught my attention.

Ziyad was shouting.

When Hahona let go of my eyes, I looked up to see we were all surrounded by familiar figures in black outfits. Wang Zi and Hahona were the first to take action. They started to shift immediately, shouting orders to us all. I saw a tiger and a jaguar take form and start to circle us. Ziyad knelt beside us, ready with his rhino horn out. In the light, it looked metallic. Clay, River, Emilia and Caaliyah were at my side helping me up and trying to get back to Clandestine, as we knew any fights within the inner grounds and building were forbidden. If you got caught, your spirit would be forcibly locked, so we needed to head back in order to survive.

Emilia tried to drag Yousef with her, but he wouldn't break form. He had these magnificent, golden glowing antlers, they were somewhat transparent, half his body also changed to take the form of a strong, black stallion and to his side, next to Ziyad, was Sebastian, in all of his spirit glory. He was larger than a regular gorilla and stood taller than all the spirits beside him.

I looked back once and saw them all break out in a fight, and all I could do was pray they didn't get injured. I closed my eyes and called to my wolves. *If you can hear me, please help me. My friends are in trouble.* I didn't know what else I could do, but it turned out that was enough, as I heard the howls echo through the night and I felt the sting of tears escaping my eyes. They had heard me.

Of course, we did, we're your pack.

I allowed my tears to fall as Tyler's voice reassured me that everything would be fine.

Tyler's POV

Ever since I had heard the McGuire family were asking questions about Mina's relationship with my brother and me, we had to put our differences aside just for the moment. Whenever the McGuire's are involved in anything, trouble always follows and it's not the good kind.

They don't have any feelings when it comes to power, it's a straight cut off. They have wanted to rule for quite some time and I wonder how aware they are of what happened to the Royals or what the connection is between Mina and them.

I saw the McGuire kid at Clandestine hovering around Nathaniel and from what I hear, he isn't aware that Mina is a therian. Neither are his family yet. However, they know she has a relationship with my brother and me and there's only so long I can keep that hidden.

If only Leo hadn't announced to the Royal circle that he wanted Mina to be his Queen, we'd have more time, but unwittingly he placed her in danger again, and now he's going out of his way to ensure that she doesn't get hurt.

Between you and me, I think he's worried I'll hide her.

The rogues were informed of Mina's group of friends; by whom, we don't know, but we will find out. They are looking for her on the grounds, so I had to make sure I was present without sounding off alarm bells, so my cover came in handy. We had a mini concert at Clandestine, which we hadn't done in a while, and it was worth it to see Mina's eyes light up because of the music I made.

The pack are also on guard, hidden just outside of the grounds, so as not to draw too much attention.

Chapter Sixteen

We got into our rooms before our paths were blocked by the students rushing out to witness all the commotion. I can't believe what had just happened. One moment we were having an amazing time and the next everything flipped over. Why were there rogues on Clandestine grounds? Did they come for me?

Emilia was pacing the length of the room and I could understand what she was going through. She had left Yousef behind, her mate. She kept playing with her hands, so I couldn't help but walk up to her and hold her hands in mine.

"Yousef will be fine, all of them will," I reassured her.

"You can't know that, did you see those rogues? There were so many. I could smell death on them from miles away, they carry the blood of the dead on their clothing, like trophies. Just thinking about it is making me crazy."

She was becoming hysterical and I wanted to tell her that it would all be fine.

"I can check for you. I'm part of the pack and I can see if I can link in, but I've never done it before." I saw a glimmer of hope in her eyes when I told her. River heard too.

"You're part of Tyler's pack?" I didn't think now was the time to get into the Luna thing.

"Something like that, but I don't know how to link in with them?" How am I still not connected to my spirit? My friends are in trouble and I can't do anything. They must have got it wrong, I might not be a therianthrope after all.

"Don't worry; Caaliyah can help you with that. She focuses me, like she did before… Mina…I'm sorry for…" River drifted into an apology and now wasn't the time.

"You didn't do anything wrong, you were sticking up for our friend. If I'd had the same opportunity I would've jumped at it too. It's my fault for getting in your way, I just didn't want you to do something that you would regret." She hugged me, which was all I needed to understand what she was feeling. I squeezed her back.

"Caaliyah, can you help me?" I asked, as she made her way to me smiling. I saw Clay move further away. There was something bothering him that I needed to talk to him about. He'd been acting weird since we were surrounded.

"Have you ever tried to connect to the pack?" Caaliyah asked.

"No, I've never tried it and I don't know how to…" Feeling pathetic about this didn't come close.

"It's okay, don't worry, I'll help you. Is there a person in the pack you connect with the most?" I nodded. I mean, come on, it's obvious. I connect with Tyler the most.

"I need you to close your eyes and focus on him, all the little things you can remember, and I'll guide you. Don't open your eyes and listen carefully. Can you all back up to the other side?" She kneeled in front of me after she ushered the others to the opposite side of the room.

Closing my eyes, I thought of Tyler, his sweet, smoky scent, the way his hair fell over his face, how I felt grounded and safe when he was around. I could hear Caaliyah talking to me, it was soothing. She asked me to try and reach him with my mind, so I let my mind focus on him, where I had left him. His voice was telling me that he could hear me. For a moment, everything went silent. I couldn't hear Caaliyah anymore and there was a jolt in me, and images flashed into my mind too fast to grasp the whole picture. I focused harder and felt myself leap into the air as the wind ruffled through my skin and the moon shone bright over my landing space.

It was Clandestine grounds. There was destruction and mayhem, wolves were everywhere, tearing into flesh, cries of agony, shouts and the cracking of bones as people were thrown around the grounds. I saw Yousef dragging Ziyad. He was hurt, both his left arm and leg were shattered as he withered in pain. Wang Zi and Hahona flanked Sebastian as they ran through the robed men, teeth wide, claws out and arms up. I watched as the robes toppled and heard the growl escape from within me as I felt a hollowed pain and centred in on it.

I saw a pale brown wolf trapped by one of the trees and a robed guy standing on his neck, claws out. I saw them reflect the light as he dug into the wolf's back and began to pull at the spine. The pain was unconceivable, and then, there was no feeling. I had no control as I flew back into the air and landed right on top of the robe, tackling him to the ground. I saw red and my teeth sank into his throat as I pulled at it, jaw clenched. The metallic taste exploded in my mouth as I stepped back.

Looking around, I counted the rest of my pack; they were okay. Wang Zi, Sebastian and Hahona ran over to Yousef and helped lift Ziyad, as they carried him in through the Clandestine doors out of sight. I walked over to the pale wolf and felt the rest of the wolves follow. Looking down I could see the pain, even though I couldn't feel anything.

Alpha please, don't leave me like this. Do it, let me go.

I felt a heaviness in my heart and turned to look at the pack and saw them all gather, compact into a tight space,

Angelico pressed down on my shoulder.

"I'm sorry, Alpha, I wish I could do this for you." His voice was a little constricted.

I turned to look down at the wolf and sighed, pulling him closer to me. He couldn't move. I kissed his head and looked into his eyes as I put both my arms around his neck and squeezed with all my strength till the light in his eyes faded. The pack howled in mourning as I let go of the wolf. He started changing back into his human form. My heart shattered, he was not much older than eighteen.

"You did what you had to, brother, it is the burden that comes with your responsibility as their leader."

"You're late; if you got here when I told you, this wouldn't have happened. I guess being King means more to you than the life of our people." Looking up, my eyes connected with Leo's.

Gasping, I felt myself being shook. My eyes opened to find River and Emilia at either side of me. That was the most surreal thing ever. I connected to Tyler and saw through him. Did he know?

"What happened? Is he okay?" Emilia was in tears.

"He's fine. Yousef isn't injured, Ziyad is. River, you're going to be needed. Go, they're here, in Clandestine. You lot go with her." Before I could finish, Emilia was out of the door. River looked back at me.

"We'll talk when I get back." She looked concerned.

"I'm okay. Go, they need you." I was exhausted. I needed to see Tyler anyway. I need to make sure he was okay; what he had to do wasn't fair.

"Are you sure you're okay? You howled, heartbroken. Is Tyler okay?" Clay moved towards me cautiously. "Tyler is fine. I didn't know I could do that. Clay, a lot of people were hurt, we lost one. I don't know what to do, I wish I could run away but I can't leave, not like this. Not after everything." Clay stood a few feet from me, what was wrong with him?

I stood up, right now I could do with a hug from my best friend. I took a step forward and he moved back, which made me freeze on the spot.

"It's not you, Mina. I need a minute. I saw you earlier, blood streaming from everywhere. I thought I was watching you die and I couldn't move. I let it go on too long. I want you to leave Clandestine; will you come with me? We don't need to go home. I just don't want to watch you keep being at the centre of danger. I can't watch anything happen to you." I understood how he felt. He thought he was losing me. My best friend was hurting, and I hadn't realised it.

I walked towards him and even though he kept backing up there was no other place he could go when he backed up to the wall. I wrapped my arms around him and placed my face firm on his chest. He took his time putting his arms around me but that was okay. I dragged him into this mess when I didn't have to; I was selfish.

"I'm sorry you had to go through that. I can't imagine what it must have felt like but, Clay, I can't leave, you know that. Right now, I need to be right here. I don't know why but there is a debt I owe to the King and I need to fulfil it. I won't ask you to stay anymore, you never asked for this and I should have said so earlier. I just thought having you with me would make life easier, but I was wrong, and it was unfair of me to do that to you." I squeezed him a little tighter hoping that he would feel my sentiments.

"Mina, I can't leave without you. I know I said I didn't want anything, and in a way I meant it, but right now, I feel like you'd be safer with me. I get that this is your world and your life right now, but it doesn't have to be. You can live away from it like many others, I just can't help but think that I at least could keep you alive away from all this. You would be safe." His voice broke and I didn't look at him. I'd never heard Clay get like this.

"I'm sorry. I can't leave, not yet." My heart was breaking for him, my best friend who'd protected me all these years. Why can I not feel something in return for him? I love Clay, I really do with all my heart. I'm just not in love with him and giving him false hope would only destroy us.

I was there for a while, putting Tyler aside for the minute, only to be disturbed with a cough. I turned around to see Tyler's eyes fixed on us for a moment and then he was gone.

The next few days, everyone was on high alert. It had gone through Clandestine that rogues had come on to the grounds and killed one of our own, a young lad named Jack Kennedy, a wolf spirit. Groups avoided us in the food hall and during classes. The triplets had told people we were the main cause of the situation and that mixing social groups brought the rogues to our doors and people lapped that up. Like seriously?

Ziyad was recovering well; Hahona and River worked with him a lot. Wang Zi, Yousef and Sebastian always walked Emilia and me to classes, and Clay never left my side. Leo was continuously checking in, even midway through lessons he would just walk in, which had everyone talking. The whispers grew louder, and people blanked me completely. On the other hand, the tutors went out of their way to support me in all subjects and that added fuel to the fire, preferential treatment. Leo just wouldn't take no for an answer and said my safety was of the upmost priority. I hadn't seen Tyler since that day. My heart ached as I couldn't comfort him when he needed me to. The big bad wolf was hurting, and he had no one to share it with.

There was one guy I could count on to still treat me the same, Cairo. He muttered at me throughout his lesson and made a scene to tell me that I may be favoured by the future king, but nothing had changed. I was still a newbie who had no say without my spirit and I had to fall in line. All the students laughed. Some joked that Leo would come for him for the demeaning remarks to his 'pet' and Cairo played them off. I didn't understand his issue with me; the guy could hold a grudge. I walked out and sat on the bench to avoid any further drama. I knew if I was in there, then Clay would have at least attempted to wipe the floor with Cairo, and that wasn't something I needed to see. Theo did his best to silence the others, but I was grateful that he had a grip on Clay. The lesson ended a lot slower than usual, time dragged, and I tried to keep it together, but my thoughts were with Tyler.

"Mina, he wants you to go in. I'll wait outside; we need to hurry so that we don't get late for the next class," Clay said as he ushered me in and closed the door. Cairo was lounging on his desk waiting for me. I tried to calm my anger at the fact that he was practically targeting me due to our first meeting. He watched as I stood in front of him and didn't speak for a few minutes.

"You like showing yourself up don't you, Mina?" His tone was so condescending that I wanted to slap him with the memoir on his desk.

"Not really, you were provoking me to react, so I left before something happened. From where I'm standing it's you who's trying to show me up every time." He just kept staring and not saying anything. I could feel my anger starting to rise and I had no control. I'm done with people thinking mistreating others for their own hidden agenda is okay.

"Do you have something to say to me or not? I have a class to get to." He stood up and walked up to me. "I just want to know why you don't care about who you are, or is it that you don't want anyone else to find out?" He lifted a strand of my hair and let it fall through his fingers, before inhaling.

"Theo was right you know, you smell lovely. You like playing pet, right? Do you want to be mine? I can be very good to you." He inhaled again but this time putting his face a little closer, and something snapped in me and my body just reacted. I shoved him, and he flew into the wall behind him, debris falling to the ground. I saw red and that was it. I had no control, walking up to him, my hand found its way to his throat. My vision had a cloudy hue, but I could sense his fear; and it felt good. It fuelled an insatiable need for satisfaction. Cairo kept mocking me, making me feel insignificant. He thought he was better. Why? Purely because he was born with a silver spoon in his mouth.

What right does any man have over another? We are all equals, prince or not, and that is something he needs to learn. No, he needs to be taught.

"Mina, you're hurting him. Look. Let him go." Clay was behind me with his arms wrapped around my waist, pulling me towards him. For a minute, I got a sense of déjà vu.

"Mina, listen to me. Look at his throat, see the blood? That's you, you're hurting him." I saw it, the red sticky pigment trickling down my hand. I immediately dropped him.

"Cairo!? I'm so sorry, I don't know what happened. Cairo, are you okay? I'm sorry. I'm so sorry." What did I do? I didn't mean to, I hurt him. Why? What is wrong with me? I could have killed him.

"Mina, it's okay. Look at me. Alexander, you need to take her to Waya as soon as you can." Clay still had his arms around me and Cairo had his hands on mine.

"Look at me, I'm okay. You don't have control and you need that before you either hurt yourself or someone else.

"I didn't know who you were. I'm sorry, forgive me." The look in his eyes was softer than it should have been.

Why isn't he angry?

"Take her to class!" Clay walked me out of Cairo's room, wiping my hands as we moved. Something in me changed. I felt it when I pushed Cairo and now in the pit of my stomach I had a dull ache, a want.

Clay's POV

Running into the room I saw Cairo land on the floor as a woman walked up to him. My eyes scanned the room for Mina, where was she? Where did this woman come from?

Her deep blue hair floated around her; the glow of her skin was something else. I'd never seen anything like it. She was lit from within and as she swayed over to Cairo, I saw recognition then fear register in his eyes. It must have been a lover's tiff.

Mina wasn't there. I turned to walk back out as I saw the claws grow from the woman's hand as she lifted Cairo by the throat and dug her claws in, the star bracelet reflected the glow from her. The star bracelet that matched the one on my wrist. I focused to look closer, beneath the blue hair, beneath the glow. I recognised my best friend.

I ran next to her in seconds, trying to pull her away from Cairo, talking her down from doing anything that would break her. As she registered what was happening, she let go and looked at me, so beautiful, the white-ish blue eyes returning to her usual brown doe-like ones, her hair going back to normal. She kneeled next to Cairo, crying, apologising. I don't even know what happened, so how can she? It seems something may have triggered her spirit.

Cairo's behaviour towards her changed completely. He told me to take Mina to Waya, whoever that is. How am I going to begin explaining this to Tyler? I'm going to have to come back to Cairo after taking Mina to her next class.

What exactly happened?

Chapter Seventeen

I could have really hurt him. Nothing could surpass the rage that I just felt, just because he used his authority as a tutor to take jabs at me all lesson. Yes, he tried to make me uncomfortable and it warranted a reaction but was I justified in attacking him? I never wanted to lose control like that again. I had to figure out how to make this transition without hurting myself or anyone else. It would help if I knew what I was letting out.

I don't know if I can class it as a plus side but when I was walking towards him, the power that pulsed through me wasn't like anything else I have ever known, it felt so good. I felt strong, not like my usual non-confrontational self. I was aware of everything, including the heart beats in that room—Cairo's, mine and Clay's. But there was one other. I sensed it, somehow trying to cloak itself in the shadows. Did Cairo have someone there to watch us?

"Mina, snap out of it," Clay shook me.

"Sorry, I…"

"Its fine, you don't need to explain. Listen to me, you can't let anyone find out what happened, Mina, so get a grip and focus· in class." His voice quivered as he fixed my clothes like a parent and then wiped the rest of the stains from my hand.

"Okay, come on, let's go…" I took his hand and walked into a large auditorium, which was different from the usual setting.

The place was enormous, divided into different areas. There was a stage at one end with theatre style seating, and on the opposite side was a full length mirrored wall, with ballet bars along it and a dance floor. Between them were the usual art groups and musicians. They were all doing their own thing, apart from one person who was furiously walking towards us. As he got closer, my heart leapt.

"Why are you late?" Tyler directed his question to Clay.

"Something came up. I need to be excused for a while." I was distracted by River coming up behind the boys. I needed a comforting hug, I opened my arms and she got the message.

"You okay?" she asked, soothingly stroking the back of my head.

"I don't know, I think I changed. I almost hurt someone, River. I don't know what to do." River squeezed me a little tighter.

"We'll talk after class." I nodded, only to be yanked from River's arms.

"Where are you hurt?" It was Tyler.

"You're hurting me." His eyes had darkened dangerously.

Clay and River tried to remove me from his grip, only for him to shove them away with an added growl.

"Tyler, don't make a scene, people are starting to watch." I saw a few of the students look at us open-mouthed. "I'm not hurt! I accidently hurt someone. Clay will explain." He mumbled an apology and something about smelling blood, as Clay led him away.

River walked me to the dance section and my heart started to panic. She reassured me that Tyler and she were the best in this area which was why they were covering for the tutor who had been taken away for an assignment. I looked back to see Clay and Tyler in a furious, animated conversation, before turning back to see Theo watching me quizzically. River took her place in front of the mirrors and talked about stretching exercises before a warm up. Theo took a spot next to me.

"You really are a trouble magnet, aren't you? First Cairo, now Tyler, what did you do?" he smirked.

"I honestly didn't do anything to either of them," I said sighing, barely able to bend into those stretches. "Well, you're becoming quite a hero. Tyler rarely blinks at us, he just walks around shouting orders and on your first day having him as a tutor, he has you in a death grip. You must've done something to annoy him." I could see a few of the others look at me as Theo pushed for answers.

"He mentioned something about being late," I answered, shrugging my shoulders. They don't need to know of my relationship with Tyler. I had enough trouble with Leo.

"That would do it; he thinks he's above everyone else. Just be careful to not get on the wrong side of him. I thought it was to do with the other Kang, Leo, his brother. They hate each other, so we all assumed he was taking things out on you. Wouldn't put it past the loser, picking on a girl." Theo came across as protective; this place needed more people like him.

The warm up was the most embarrassing thing I had ever experienced. I was out of breath within five minutes, literally gasping for air. I would've much preferred being chased by men in robes than face the weird looks of amusement I'd received from the rest of the class. Theo came over and handed me some water, rubbing my back as though that would help. Can't blame the kid for trying, surprisingly it didn't feel odd. I watched Tyler saunter around the place. His hair was down, and he was wearing a beige sleeveless vest with perfectly placed holes. He wore his jeans dark and fitted, showing his thigh muscles as he moved. Girls fluttered their lashes and lowered their shirts, so that he could get a glimpse. Unintentionally, I growled and his eyes caught mine and darkened. He then looked to Theo and started to storm towards us.

"What was that growl for? I'm only trying to help," Theo laughed.

"It wasn't aimed at you, more the fact that I have to make an idiot out of myself to stay here," I said standing up.

"You can't connect with your spirit, I'm guessing?" I nodded in response to his question.

"Don't worry, you'll get the hang of it. I struggle to contain my wolf at times and I hate phasing, it hurts. It's not like I wanted this, but…" He trailed off, not wanting to continue in the direction he was going.

"Well, at least you know who you are," I smiled, trying to change the mood.

Tyler was right behind him and his face didn't look good. I missed his face. I'd not seen him since the other night and my mind had progressed from thinking about comforting him to kissing him. Not the usual way my mind works, but something had changed from when I was linked to him. I'm more connected. I had to bite back a groan at the thought. Tyler took a step back. *Don't worry, I'll try not to jump on you, I don't like an audience,* I thought and saw him raise his brow at me. There was also the hint of a smirk that woke up the butterflies in my stomach that had been dormant since his performance.

"You're that out of breath? Do you even work out?" Yup the moment's gone, I wanted to smack his face.

"I do actually work out; it's just been a while since the last time, not that it's any of your business!" I said scowling, not caring that everyone else had stopped warming up because of Tyler's presence.

"That's no excuse for stopping, work through it," he stated. He knew how to put a girl down.

"Tyler, I didn't realise you had an interest in dance. Can you not disturb my students unless you want to join us for the next bit, we are partnering up?" River, my knight.

"Sure, I'll partner with…" Tyler looked at me like he was ready for round two, only to be cut off by Theo.

"River, I'm partnering with Mina. I know I can help her and she's new to dance, so she's uncomfortable but knows me." Theo took my hand to lead me to the floor with the rest of them, only to be blocked by Tyler, which attracted the attention of the other kids.

Theo placed me behind him as he squared up to Tyler. It would have been heroic if I didn't know Tyler had a temper, so it seemed a little more idiotic. I tried to get between them only to be held in place by Theo.

"Who are you little man?" Tyler asked amused, standing over him, almost laughing.

"I'm her Teddy!" Theo's remark didn't go down well, and before I knew it, Tyler had lifted him off the ground by his collar. I somehow got between the boys, which wasn't easy. Then, placing my hand on Tyler, I asked him to let go, and much to my surprise he did.

"I have a lot to learn," I said, pulling Theo towards the floor. *Stop being an idiot, he's a kid.* River tried to usher Tyler off, but he wasn't having any of it, and didn't take his eyes off Theo for a second. I heard the other students whisper things between themselves, like:

Who does she think she is!
Did you see that?
Who is she?

Are they both crazy, don't they know Tyler?
She just skipped out on a once-in-a-lifetime opportunity.
I would kill to partner with him.
Why her? She's not even pretty.

"Don't listen to them, they're jealous. You are pretty and they're just annoyed that Tyler wanted to partner with you. But don't worry, I won't let him mess you about." Theo just smiled.

"You tell me not to get on his wrong side and look at what you go and do. You should've just let him partner with me." I smiled, rolling my eyes.

He led me through class well; I barely had to do anything. Tyler eventually moved away and did what he was supposed to, but it didn't help that we had put him in a bad mood. He scowled and shouted the whole session. I waited back for River after class, she was collecting her equipment and paperwork as I came up behind her. Tyler was tidying up behind the stage somewhere. I needed some lunch and a chat about what happened with Cairo, the session had completely drained me.

"You could have told me that you teach this class, it would have been so much easier for me coming in here," I said, giving her a hug.

"I thought I would surprise you," she laughed.

"Uh huh," I replied, looking to see if Tyler had come out yet.

"Can we reschedule lunch today?" she asked.

"What, why?" She would never reschedule on me.

"I think he needs you more today," she replied, nodding towards the theatre as I walked her out.

"Who?" I asked, trying not to let my happiness show on my face.

"Seriously? You're gonna try that with me?" I laughed to hide my embarrassment.

"It's not his fault he's in a mood today. He's been tracking some rogues and is in a bad shape." My heart sunk; he'd been injured again. Was it because of me?

"I will have you excused from the rest of the day. Only Tyler and I have a key to this hall, I'm going to lock it from the outside and I'll distract Leo. Don't look at me like that. I know there's something there. I can see it on your face." What would I do without this girl?

She handed me a neat box as she locked the door behind her. I sent a quick message to Clay, telling him I'd see him later in the evening. My heart started to race as I thought of Tyler and I locked up in here for the rest of the day. Putting my stuff down, I opened the box to find some sandwiches and cut fruit. I poured two glasses of water from the dispensers and took them backstage.

Tyler had his hair tied up in a knot and was fixing one of the lights. A few strands fell over his face, touching his lips, and the light really accentuated his beauty. That's the guy I once kissed.

Tyler stopped what he was doing but didn't come off the ladder. I guess he was angry at me for hugging Clay when he needed me, or maybe he didn't trust that I wouldn't leap on him.

"It's me I don't trust. Not you." I looked at him and saw that his eyes told me exactly what he meant.

Tyler's POV

She came in looking a little upset, and with the stench of blood, I couldn't contain my anger when I thought she was hurt. From the moment we kissed, she sealed my fate. I knew we're meant to be together, but she lost all control. I can't put her in a situation where her judgment is clouded; I can't take her like that. I'm in even less control around her, I can't fight my urge to mate and she makes it that much more difficult. When she nipped my lip, I felt it, her desire, it filled my body. If Clay hadn't taken her off me back then, we would have been unable to stop.

I've been around women, but none like her. She can buckle me with a single kiss. Even now, in a hall full of people, I can only see her. Her thoughts don't help the situation. I don't know how much longer I can hold myself back. She's not ready. Her thoughts are increasing the pheromones in her scent, which isn't a good thing when Clandestine is filled with unmated males. I won't always be around to keep them away.

Do I mate or not?

Chapter Eighteen

His words multiplied the butterflies in my stomach. I needed to shake off this feeling or I wouldn't be able to control it anymore.

"Can you stop thinking like that?!" he sounded exasperated, like it was my fault.

"How am I meant to control what I think? This means something different to me, you wouldn't understand." I hated physical contact but with Tyler, he made me want to revel in the feeling. It was new to me, I liked the way he made me feel.

"Mina, stop!" Tyler was gripping the ladder, his knuckles white. Even the veins in his hands, running up his forearm, were attractively enticing me. I'm losing it!

Tyler started laughing, so deeply and infectiously it made me laugh with him. Why is there beauty in everything of his? *Don't get a big head; I can't help the way you make me feel.* I thought as he grinned at me, earning him a roll of the eye.

"Come down from there, I'm not gonna eat you. Have some lunch." Finally, he came down, wiped down a bench so that I could sit down and sat next to me. So chivalrous.

I tried not to smile as I sneaked a look at his pretty face, but I knew he was reading my thoughts as a smiled formed on his lips to mirror mine. I couldn't help myself, I reached out and tucked the escaped strands of his hair behind his ear.

"Jeez, Mina, you make me feel like I'm all delicate. Stop doing stuff like that." I just blankly stared.

"I was trying to be nice, it's not my fault you feel like that. It's what you get for being too pretty. Princess!" I tried to wiggle my eyebrows at him, but he covered my face with his palm and gave it a little shove backwards and I thought he better not have smudged my brows or makeup.

"Stop calling me princess, or I might just use a wet wipe," he laughed.

"I can't, I like it. It can be our secret?!" I had to be careful not to disturb his macho alpha image in front of the pack or his stonehearted image in front of the other kids. But when we were alone, just us, he can be my princess, can't he?

"Trust me, I'm not a princess," he said, taking a huge bite out of his sandwich, distracting me with his jaw line. He even eats hot. Here I am with crumbs all over my clothes. Looking down, I realise I needed to remove them. Tyler choked, spitting out food, shocking me. I gave him some water and smacked his back as he got over it.

"Are you okay?" I asked after he regained his composure.

"I'm fine, can you keep your thoughts clean?" Clean? I didn't even think about him.

"You said you want to take your clothes off," he replied to my thought.

"No, I didn't! I wouldn't even say that, what do you take me for?" What the heck, I didn't even think about that. He's insane, I'm not going to bare any of my skin next to his perfectness. I don't even think I've shaved my legs and underarms, not that if I had I'd show him. Oh… I get it.

"I meant take the crumbs off my clothes, stupid, not my clothes. You need help if your thoughts are that far into the gutter." It's funny, even though that's not what I meant, his reaction was perfect. It's all new and interesting.

"What's interesting?" he asked.

"You! How you make me feel." It took years for me to let Jesse get close enough to even kiss or cuddle me, and it never went beyond that, and when Leo kissed me the other day I basically regurgitated my entire stomach content but with Tyler I wanted to pursue him, which is a first for me, and his kiss sent tingles through me like electricity. I wanted more of them.

"He did what?" Tyler jumped off his seat and was freaking out.

"What?" Who?

"You kissed my brother?" Uh oh.

"It wasn't liked that, it kinda happened and I didn't know how to fight it. It was once. I'm sorry." Wait, why was I apologising when it wasn't my fault? It was before I met him.

"You need to stop invading my thoughts or you'll hear things you don't like," I scowled.

"I can't help it, I want to know everything. I never knew what you felt before and now I know, I can't help it. Listening in on what you think of me, has now become an addiction. I enjoy it, dangerously so, you always have me on edge." He was cute, unfortunately for me, like he needed further attributes to set us apart.

"You don't get it, do you, Mina? I've loved you from the moment I first laid eyes on you; you're the most beautiful girl I've come across. In the past, I misunderstood you a lot and I left thinking you were happier without me. I almost lost you, I won't make that mistake again. I know how you feel about me and I'm going to keep my promise." He was talking faster than normal and a lot more animated than I'd ever seen before. I couldn't help but smile.

He came and kneeled by my feet, taking my hands in his and just stared at me. He's not going to propose right? I might just say yes. Erm wait, that's not what I meant.

"Too late, you want to marry me? You want me that much, huh?" My leg reacted by itself. I kicked his shin and he was on the floor. I feigned an 'oops'.

"That's what you get for being too cocky. Yes, I like you and just as easily I can unlike you too. I'm only fascinated by this because I thought I was abnormal. I usually hate physical contact from people pursuing me." Serves him right, I wished I could contain my thoughts and emotions around him; it was definitely something to get used to and I liked it. I couldn't hide my smile.

"You can unlike me huh? That easily?" Tyler was facing me, his hands perched on either side of the bench with me trapped between. His gaze sent my heart into a wild rhythm, he's too close and looking too intently. His hair fell down his face. As he tried to blow it out of the way, I reached up and tucked it back behind his ear, only this time my hands lingered as they came down his jaw. I heard his heart beat loud and clear in the silence, it matched mine perfectly. I make him as nervous as he made me. Who can win this game?

"I can win, sweetheart, trust me!" Seriously? I might be new to this whole feelings and tension stuff but I don't lose to anyone; I especially do not want to lose to Tyler. His scent tickled my senses and his close proximity only pushed my imagination further.

I leant in closer. He can already anticipate all my moves, so does it matter if I think about kissing him? His jawline, down his neck, his Adams apple. How would the shadow of his stubble feel against my lips or my neck? I heard him bite down a growl; biting my bottom lip, I fight my own.

"What do you want, Tyler?" I whispered inches from his lips.

"Do you know why you thought there was something wrong with you, why you hate contact from the male specimen who show an interest in you? Have you not figured it out yet?" He seemed elated, and it fuelled my own happiness as I understood his question all too clearly.

"Because to begin with, I was tied to you?" My mouth hurt from smiling too much. I had subconsciously blocked guys out because he's my mate. I knew it. Or my spirit knew it from the very beginning.

"You weren't tied to me but that can be arranged," he said, laughing brightly.

"You avoided my question, what do you want from me Tyler?" I said smiling against his cheek. He pushed me back so he could look at me.

"I want you, Mina, all of you from the way you scrunch your nose to the way you get annoyed at me. I want to wake up every day knowing that we are finally together after all these years of me chasing you. More than that, I want you happy and give you everything you want and more, especially me."

"Mina, you were always mine. I didn't know, all these years."

He lifted me off the bench which earned him a squeal of delight. I couldn't stop giggling as my legs wrapped around his waist and he nuzzled his face into my ribs. I guess we were both on the same page. I kissed his forehead and he looked up at me, eyes glistening.

"You better not start crying, princess; I don't know how to deal with man tears," I said laughing.

"I'm not crying! You better not tell anyone I was crying!" he said, shaking his head furiously. I couldn't help myself, I'd not seen this side to a guy, nor had I thought I'd see this side to Tyler. He's always tried to irritate me, but the guy had happy tears, and for some reason it filled my heart with an unsubstantial amount of joy. I wanted to love him, care for him and protect him. I held his face, so he couldn't shake it anymore and gave his cheeks a pinch, pulling him closer to plant a kiss on his lips. I would love him with everything I had.

"I love you, Mina. I have always loved you." His words changed this whole world. I can deal with it all, the shapeshifting, the rogues, the throne with Leo, my spirit. I can take it all on as long as I have him.

As I was about to tell him I felt the same, he became unbalanced. He looked at me, his eyes changed from showing love to something else. They had a faraway look as he fell to his knees with me in his arms.

"Tyler, Tyler what's wrong? Tyler?" He wasn't answering. His eyes were transfixed on me and I saw fear, before he opened his mouth. I looked down to see a metal rod sticking out of him, what happened? We were alone, we were fine. What happened?!

"Tyler please... please." Shaking him, I couldn't understand or make sense of what was happening. The door was locked. We were alone. He loves me; we made progress. How did he end up with a metal rod in him? Who else is here? All these questions invaded my head.

My vision started to blur, I felt weird. Someone had tried to take what's mine, someone had tried to hurt Tyler. My head became heavy and cloudy, and anger surged through my body. There was an intense ringing in my ears that grew louder, giving me an ear-splitting headache and making me unstable. I was shaking, what do I do? How do I save him?

I was finally able to sense the presence of someone else, in my inner chaos. They're here but I can't see them. "Show yourself, you coward!" I said, looking around but making sure I was close to Tyler's limp body. The situation was all too familiar and real for me to comprehend my inability to take in enough oxygen that would prevent me from hyperventilating. I wouldn't let anything happen to him.

I placed myself over his body. It was a long shot but if I could make sure that nothing further happened to him, maybe he would heal. Flashbacks from the past, of my dreams pierced my mind. He risked his life for me, surely I can do the same for him? I knew the pull I felt towards him was real and I wouldn't ever get that again. If he goes, I should too; that's the choice he'd always made.

I felt my legs crack and the immensity of the pain made me let out a scream, which was covered by an earthshattering growl that filled me with dread. I can't let him be taken away. The pain in my legs was making me delirious and I started hallucinating. I could see multiple bodies in the room, only the doors are locked. There's no one here but us and the one who's trying to kill him. Tyler, lying beneath me, was pale and cold. He was going to die. I'd only just tasted happiness, for a second. I couldn't let him go.

The rod was in the way. I couldn't even get close to him, to warm him up. Blood coloured the floor red and everything around us was crashing down. I heard the growls from all around me. I couldn't let fear and delusions take over, no one could have him, not without me. I didn't know what I was thinking, but the only way was this—if they wanted him they could have me too. The growls intensified and I heard them closer. I couldn't make out if they were real, but I could hear howls too, emotional ones. Ones that hurt me, painful and distressing. I felt a sudden rush of air around me and realised this could be it, the moment I lose him, my mate. I accepted my fate. I'm sorry mum, dad, Clay, River and Leo, I can't be without him. Not now. Inhaling, I lifted the top part of my body and forced myself onto Tyler, feeling the metal rod pierce through me, nauseating me. It's done, the pain, I can't comprehend it. It's like I'm drowning in metallic water, unable to breathe as my throat closes up and tears sting my eyes. I hear them.

"Luna stop! Alpha!" A little too late.

"Mina, what happened?! What did you do to her?" It was the heart-wrenching sound of Clay's tear stricken voice.

I'm so sorry, I had no choice. I finally found someone who completes me, someone who I forgot and left behind.

I took his love for granted. I'm sorry, forgive me for causing you pain, but I can't leave him ever again. Succumbing to the pain, I saw everything clearly. Tyler protected me with his life always. He put me first, he loved me in ways that I never thought possible. I remember everything that he promised and everything he sacrificed, all he didn't know, it was all coming back to me in those last few moments. I was scared; I didn't want to die. I didn't want to leave everyone. Please not now, not when I know who I was and who I promised my father I would be, I know that I'm the last Royal, my father's secret child. The pain of remembering my lost loved ones was tearing every inch of my heart apart, I remembered too late. Father, I didn't complete your promise, I can't protect our people. My eyes were too heavy, everything was slowing down, I was cold. Closing my eyes, I whispered, hoping he could hear me, "I love you, Tyler, I always will…"

Clay's POV

Waya had some interesting information about how Mina was before the incident that brought her to me. I needed to get Mina to him as soon as possible. She needs to learn the truth of her capabilities and how awesome she was and still is; she needed that boost of confidence to find her feet.

Getting to the auditorium I saw some guys from the pack running through the doors. The lights were all out in the corridor. As I hurried towards the door, the ground tremored forcefully beneath my feet, making me stumble. The power was magnetic, holding me to the ground.

I could hear the guys inside shout for Mina.

Mina!

Dragging myself off the floor I run into the hall, only to find everyone backing away from the collapsed stage. In the centre, I could make out two figures covered in blood and my heart sank as I instantly recognised my best friend in all her ethereal glory lying on top of Tyler. Her blue hair sprawled over him and a metal rod holding the pair together. Her silver eyes see me, as the weight of the image before me brought me to my knees.

I shouldn't have left her side.